哈福

哈福

美國老師教你
輕鬆說英語

我們的任務是使每位學英語的人,都能「學**最純正、最常用**的英語!」所以,本書的對話,都是生活中自然純正的美式英語會話。

會話超簡單,方便開口說
學習好輕鬆,隨學又隨用

天天開心說英文

附 MP3

施孝昌◎著

輕鬆有趣，隨心所欲

Fast & Easy!

本書是您學好英語的秘密武器。會話超簡單，方便開口說，學習好輕鬆，隨學又隨用。長駐美國，英語老師傳講好英語的 6 個秘訣。英語會話 Speed Up! 悠哉悠哉說，自然建立訓練英語自信心！

每一個學習英語的人，最大的希望是什麼？那就是能以英語適切、流利地表達自己的意見，用英語與人溝通、與人洽談生意。換句話說，不論是在公司上班、出國、談生意或結交朋友，只要是需要用到英語的場合，您一定希望輕鬆愉快地開口暢談。

為了幫助您達成這個心願，特別製作這套書，完全根據人類學習外語的學習過程來編寫，都是模擬外國人每天說的話，你在我們所製作的英語書裡，所學到每一句英語，都可以隨時用來跟外國人說，外國人一定聽得懂，每一句話保證都是非常實用道地，我們要你天天聽，時時聽，有空就聽，聽了之後，你就得跟著說，那如果聽不懂，怎麼跟著說呢？

所以，我們錄製 MP3 時，都會先用慢慢的速度念，我們要求美籍老師慢慢唸的原因就是，要讓你模仿外國老師的語調，把每一句會話都能說得跟外國人一樣。

初學英語，講起話來，總覺得呆板、冗長，這不全然是缺乏練習，而是缺乏情境，一個完全美式生活的語言情境。本書提供鮮活情境會話，將生活化的美語情境，呈現在你面前。你會發現，原來原味鮮活的美語，竟是意想不到的輕鬆、簡單，讓你說起美語，頓時活靈活現。

　　和老外聊天聊什麼最好？運動、健身、休閒、生活、休假旅遊、興趣嗜好，都是簡單熱門，不褪流行的新鮮話題。無論您身處辦公室、學校或任何社交場合、豐富充足的美語話題，能讓您左右逢源，無往不利。對話新奇活潑，詳述美國風俗，是您迅速交友，學好英文的隨身手冊。

　　本書最大特色：單字很簡單，句子最簡短，會話超簡單，方便開口說，學習好輕鬆，隨學又隨用，內容輕鬆又有趣，說英語可以隨心所欲，讀完本書，保證讓您天天開心說英文。依據本書設計，按部就班學習，您自然可以達成說流利英語的終極目標。每天 10 分鐘，你的進步連老外都會大吃一驚。

　　　　　　　　　作者　　謹識

前言 **輕鬆有趣，隨心所欲**

Chapter 1

見面打招呼

朋友間打招呼

MP3-2

Conversation 1:

A: Hey Mary!
（嗨，瑪麗。）

B: Oh, hi.
（噢，嗨。）

I didn't see you there.
（我沒看到你。）

A: How've you been?
（你最近好嗎？）

B: Good.
（很好。）

I just got a new job.
（我剛找到一個新工作。）

A: Really?
（真的？）

B: Yah, I'm working at The Pizza Hut.
（是的，我在必勝客比薩餅店工作。）

A: What's up?

（有什麼新鮮事？）

B: Not much.

（沒有。）

What's up with you?

（你呢？）

A: I'm on my way to work.

（我正要去上班。）

B: I thought this was your day off.

（我以為今天你休假。）

A: It is, but Amy called in sick.

（是的，但是，艾米請了病假。）

They wanted me there an hour ago.

（他們一個小時之前叫我去上班。）

B: You'd better run then.

（那你最好快點。）

See you.

（再見。）

A: How's it going?

B: Not too bad.

> **A:** 最近怎麼樣？
>
> **B:** 還好。

A: Howdy.

B: Hey, how are you?

> **A:** 你好。
>
> **B:** 嗨，你好嗎？

A: See you later.

B: Hang in there.

> **A:** 再見。
>
> **B:** 保重。

A: Take care.

B: Okay.

See you tomorrow.

> **A:** 保重 。
>
> **B:** 好的。
>
> 明天見。

單字

job	[dʒɑb]	工作
really	[ˈriəlɪ]	真的
thought	[θɔt]	想（think 的過去式）；認為
ago	[əˈgo]	在 ... 之前
later	[ˈletɚ]	稍後

Unit

2 認識新朋友

MP3-3

Conversation 1:

A: Hi, my name is Sally.

（嗨，我名叫莎莉。）

B: I'm Tony.

（我叫湯尼。）

A: Are you new in town?

（你是新來的嗎？）

B: Yep, I just moved in the other day.

（是的，我前幾天剛搬來。）

A: Good.

（好。）

I live on the corner so come by if you need any help.

（我就住在轉角處，如果有需要幫忙，隨時過來。）

B: Thanks, I will.

（謝謝你，我會的。）

A: How are you?

（你好嗎？）

B: Fine.

（很好。）

I hope this class will be good.

（我希望這門課上得好。）

A: Me too.

（我也是這麼希望。）

I don't guess we've ever met.

（我不認為我們見過面。）

I'm Scott.

（我叫史考特。）

B: Nice to meet you.

（很高興見到你。）

I'm Mary.

（我叫瑪麗。）

A: Is this your first semester?

（這是你的第一學期課嗎？）

B: Yah.

（是的。）

In fact, you're the first person I've met on campus.

（事實上，你是我來學校認識的第一個人。）

A: I'm John, and you are?

B: My name is Mary.

> **A:** 我叫約翰，你呢？
>
> **B:** 我叫瑪麗。

A: Hello, my name is Mary.

B: Nice to meet you.

I'm John.

> **A:** 哈囉，我名叫瑪麗。
>
> **B:** 很高興見到你。

A: Hey, how's it going?

I'm John.

B: I'm Mary.

> **A:** 嗨，你好嗎？
>
> 我叫約翰。
>
> **B:** 我叫瑪麗。

A: Have we met before?

B: No, I don't think so.

I'm Mary.

A: 我們見過面嗎？

B: 沒有，我們沒見過面。

我叫瑪麗。

單字

town	[taʊn]	城市；城鎮
corner	[ˈkɔrnɚ]	n. 角落
guess	[gɛs]	猜想
met	[mɛt]	見面；見過面（meet 的過去式、過去分詞）
meet	[mit]	見面
semester	[səˈmɛstɚ]	學期
campus	[ˈkæmpəs]	校園

朋友要搬家

MP3-4

Conversation 1:

A: I'm sad that you are moving.

（你要搬家我很難過。）

B: I know.

（我知道。）

I'm kind of sad, too.

（我也是有點難過。）

A: Do you think you can come back to visit?

（你想你會回來看我們嗎？）

B: Sure, but only a couple of times a year.

（當然囉，但是，一年只能兩三次。）

A: Well, you make sure to call me when you come.

（好吧，你回來的時候，一定要打電話給我。）

B: I will.

（我會的。）

I'll send you my email address when I get there, too.

（我到的時候，會把我的電子郵件地址給你。）

Conversation 2:

A: So tomorrow's the big move, huh?

（明天就是搬家的大日子了。）

B: Yep.

（是啊。）

I can't believe it's already here.

（我真不敢相信真是時候了。）

A: Me neither.

（我也是。）

I'm going to miss you.

（我會想念你。）

B: Do you want to come see me off tomorrow?

（明天你會來道別嗎？）

A: I'd better just say bye now.

（我最好現在跟你說再見。）

Call me, okay?

（記得要打電話給我。）

B: I will.

（我會的。）

Thanks for everything you've done.

（謝謝你為我所做的一切。）

I'm going to miss you.

（我會想念你。）

More Practices:

A: I'm going to miss you.

B: I'll miss you too.

A: 我會想念你。

B: 我也會想念你。

A: Will you write me when you're gone?

B: You bet, but you'd better write me back.

A: 你走了之後，會寫信給我嗎？

B: 會的，你可要回信。

A: I wish you didn't have to move.

B: I know, but it's for the best.

A: 我希望你不要搬家。

B: 我知道，但是這是最好的。

A: Keep in touch.

B: I will.

I'll e-mail you.

A: 要保持聯繫。

B: 我會的。

我會寫電子郵件給你。

單字

sad	[sæd]	悲傷的
move	[muv]	搬家
back	[bæk]	回來
visit	['vɪzɪt]	v. 訪問；拜訪
sure	[ʃʊr]	a. 確定
send	[sɛnd]	寄；送
address	[ə'drɛs]	n. 地址
believe	[bɪ'liv]	v. 相信
neither	['niðɚ]	兩者皆不
miss	[mɪs]	v. 想念
tomorrow	[tə'maro]	明天
touch	[tʌtʃ]	聯絡

Conversation 1:

A: How's it going?
（你好嗎？）

B: Good.
（很好。）

Are you enjoying the party?
（你在這個宴會玩得愉快嗎？）

A: Yah, it's great.
（很愉快。）

B: Who did you come with?
（你跟誰一起來？）

A: Susan.
（蘇珊。）

B: I'd like to meet her.
（介紹我跟她認識吧。）

Conversation 2:

A: Thanks for coming by.
（謝謝你們來。）

B: Thanks for having us.

（謝謝你邀請我們。）

A: Did you have a good time?

（你們玩得愉快嗎？）

B: Yah, this was the best party I've been to in a long time.

（是的，這是很久以來我參加的最好的一次宴會。）

A: Well, I'm glad to hear that.

（很高興聽到你這麼說。）

B: See you around.

（再見。）

More Practices:

A: Great party, huh?

B: Yah, it's fun to meet people.

　　A: 很棒的宴會。

　　B: 是啊，來認識一些人真不錯。

A: Are you enjoying the party?

B: Yah.

I'm Scott.

I don't guess we've met.

　　A: 你玩得愉快嗎？

　　B: 很愉快。

我叫史考特。

我不認為我們見過面。

A: Hey, I'm John.

Some party, eh?

B: It's all right.

> **A:** 嗨，我叫約翰。
>
> 真是不錯的宴會。
>
> **B:** 還好。

A: I'm Charles.

Would you like to dance?

B: No thanks, I came with my husband.

> **A:** 我叫查理。
>
> 要跳個舞嗎？
>
> **B:** 不，謝謝你，我跟我先生一起來。

單字

enjoy	[ɪnˈdʒɔɪ]	喜歡；感到樂趣
party	[ˈpɑrtɪ]	宴會；派對
fun	[fʌn]	好玩；樂趣
dance	[dæns]	v. 跳舞
husband	[ˈhʌzbənd]	丈夫

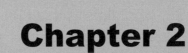

Chapter 2

跟陌生人閒聊

在公車站

Conversation 1:

A: So, what time is this bus supposed to get here?

（公車什麼時候應該到站？）

B: Who knows?!

（誰知道？）

A: Do you ride the bus often?

（你常搭公車嗎？）

B: No, just about every week or two.

不常，一、兩個星期搭一次。

A: This is my first time.

（這是我第一次搭。）

My car broke down.

（我的車子壞了。）

B: Oh, I'm sorry to hear that.

（噢，我很替你難過。）

Conversation 2:

A: Do you ride the bus often?

（你常搭公車嗎？）

B: Yep, every day.

（是的，我每天搭。）

A: Huh, I'm surprised I haven't seen you before.

（我很驚訝，我以前沒見過你。）

I'm John.

（我叫約翰。）

B: I'm Mary.

（我叫瑪麗。）

I don't ride this bus every day, but I do ride a bus every day.

（我沒有每天搭這般公車，但是我確實是每天搭公車。）

A: Oh, I see.

（噢，原來是這樣。）

B: Yah, I usually ride the bus that runs down 5th street.

（是的，我通常都搭往第五號街那班公車。）

More Practices:

A: First time on the bus?

B: Yah.

    A: 你第一次搭公車嗎？

    B: 是的。

A: Riding the bus sure is nice, huh?

B: I think so.

> **A:** 搭公車真不錯。
>
> **B:** 是啊。

A: I don't guess I've ever seen you on this bus before.

Are you new around here?

B: No, I just decided to take the bus today.

> **A:** 我不認為我以前在這班公車上見過你。
>
> 你是新來的嗎？
>
> **B:** 不是，我今天想要搭公車。

A: Do you think the bus will be by soon?

B: Yah, it usually comes at 2:10.

> **A:** 你想公車很快會到嗎？
> **B:** 是的，它通常在兩點十分到。

單字

supposed	[sə'pozd]	（口語）應該
ride	[raɪd]	搭乘
surprised	[sə'praɪzd]	訝異的；驚訝的
usually	['juʒʊəlɪ]	adv. 通常
street	[strit]	街道
decide	[dɪ'saɪd]	v. 決定

在電梯裡

Conversation 1:

A: Going up?

（往上嗎？）

B: Yes, 5th floor please.

（是的，我要去五樓。）

A: 5th floor it is.

（五樓。）

How are you today?

（你今天好嗎？）

B: Okay, but I feel like I've been running around all day.

（還好，但是我感覺整天都到處跑。）

A: Oh, one of those days.

（噢，有時就是這樣。）

B: You can say that again.

（是啊。）

A: What floor?

（到幾樓？）

B: 14.

（十四樓。）

Thanks.

（謝謝。）

A: Don't you work for John Smith?

（你不是替約翰史密斯工作嗎？）

B: Yes, as a matter of fact I do.

（是的。）

A: I'm his brother.

（我是他哥哥。）

I thought I recognized you.

（我想我認識你。）

My name is Robert.

（我名叫羅伯。）

B: All right.

（是啊。）

I thought I recognized you, too.

（我想我也認出你了。）

Small world.

（這世界真小。）

A: What floor?

B: 4 please.

> **A:** 到幾樓？）
>
> **B:** 到四樓。

A: Are you going down?

B: No, I'm going up.

> **A:** 你要下去嗎？
>
> **B:** 不，我要往上。

A: Could you hold the elevator, please?

B: You bet.

> **A:** 你可以暫停電梯嗎？
>
> **B:** 可以。

A: Can you hit the 8th floor for me?

B: There you go.

> **A:** 請你替我按八樓。
>
> **B:** 好的。

單字

floor	[flor]	樓層
feel	[fil]	感覺
again	[ə'gen]	再度；又

recognize	[ˈrɛkəgˌnaɪz]	認得；認出
small	[smɔl]	小的
world	[wɝld]	n. 世界
elevator	[ˈɛləˌvetɚ]	電梯
hit	[hɪt]	按

在學校的自助餐廳

MP3-8

Conversation 1:

A: How are you?

（你好嗎？）

B: Fine.

（很好。）

What do you think of this lunch?

（你認為午餐怎麼樣？）

A: I don't know.

（不知道。）

It looks pretty scary to me.

（看起來很可怕。）

B: Are you going to eat it?

（你要吃嗎？）

A: I guess so.

（還是要吃。）

What else am I going to do?

（還有什麼別的可以吃呢？）

B: Good point.

（你説的有理。）

Conversation 2:

A: Looks pretty good today, huh?

（今天的食物看起來不錯。）

B: Yah, but that's relative.

（是的，但那只是比較起來不錯。）

A: What do you mean?

（你是什麼意思？）

B: Well, good for the cafeteria doesn't necessarily mean that it's going to taste good.

（以餐廳的食物來説是不錯，但不代表就好吃。）

A: I see what you mean.

（我懂你的意思。）

B: Yah, it's all relative.

（是的，都是比較起來看的。）

More Practices:

A: Looks good today, huh?

B: I'd say so.

    A: 今天的食物看起來不錯。

    B: 是的。

A: Do you think that salad looks good?

B: Not really.

I'm not much on salad.

> **A:** 你認為沙拉好嗎？
>
> **B:** 不怎麼樣。
>
> 我不太喜歡沙拉。

A: How much is an extra vegetable?

B: I think it's 50 cents.

> **A:** 多一份蔬菜要多少錢？
>
> **B:** 我想是五角吧。

A: Do they let you get seconds?

B: No, not unless you want to pay for it.

> **A:** 他們允許你拿第二份嗎？
>
> **B:** 不行，除非你再另外付錢。

單字

pretty	['prɪtɪ]	adv. 非常；相當
scary	['skɛrɪ]	恐怖的
point	[pɔɪnt]	n. 要點；重點
relative	['rɛlətɪv]	比較的
cafeteria	[ˌkæfə'tɪrɪə]	自助餐廳
necessarily	['nɛsəsɛrɪlɪ]	必然的
mean	[min]	意思是

taste	[test]	v. 嚐起來
extra	[ˈɛkstrə]	額外的；多餘的
vegetable	[ˈvɛdʒtəbl̩]	蔬菜
unless	[ənˈlɛs]	除非
pay	[pe]	付錢

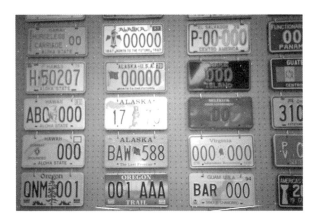

Chapter 3

跟熟識的朋友聊天

談彼此認識的朋友

MP3-9

Conversation 1:

A: What's Andy up to?

（安迪最近怎麼樣？）

B: He's working on a new computer.

（他在組一部新電腦。）

A: Oh, did he get the other one done?

（噢，他另一部組完了嗎？）

B: Yes, he finally just finished working on it.

（是的，他終於把它組好了。）

Conversation 2:

A: Hey John.

（嗨，約翰。）

B: What's going on?

（你最近在做什麼？）

A: Oh, I'm just working on some projects.

（噢，我在忙一些學校的研究報告。）

B: I see.

（是這樣。）

Have you heard from Mary today?

（你最近有瑪麗的消息嗎？）

A: Yeah, she said to tell you that she's coming over at 5.

（有，她要我告訴你她五點要過來。）

B: Good, I couldn't get a hold of her.

（很好，我一直聯絡她不上。）

More Practices:

A: How's John doing?

B: Not too good.

He's got the flu.

A: 約翰好嗎？

B: 不太好。

他患了流行性感冒。

A: Have you heard from Michael?

B: No, I haven't.

A: 你最近有沒有邁可的消息？

B: 沒有。

A: What do you think John is up to?

B: Probably just working.

> **A:** 你想約翰最近在做什麼？
>
> **B:** 可能就是在上班。

A: Have you talked to Tom recently?

B: Yeah, he's working up at Pizza Inn now.

> **A:** 你最近有沒有跟湯姆說過話？
>
> **B:** 有，他現在在比薩客棧工作。

單字

computer	[kəmˈpjutɚ]	n. 電腦
finally	[ˈfaɪnlɪ]	最終；終於
finish	[ˈfɪnɪʃ]	完成
project	[ˈprɑdʒɛkt]	專案；企畫；學校研究作業
heard	[hɝd]	聽見（hear 的過去式）
probably	[ˈprɑbəblɪ]	或許；可能的
recently	[ˈrisn̩tlɪ]	最近地

Conversation 1:

A: Did you hear that I'm going to the opera tonight?

（你有沒有聽說我今晚要去聽歌劇？）

B: Are you kidding?

（你在開玩笑嗎？）

A: No, Mary talked me into it.

（沒有開玩笑，瑪麗說服我去的。）

B: I hope you don't fall asleep.

（我希望你別睡著。）

A: Me too.

（我也是。）

I'd rather watch the hockey game.

（我寧願看曲棍球比賽。）

B: Of course you would.

（當然囉。）

Who wouldn't?

（誰不喜歡看曲棍球比賽？）

A: Did you hear about John and Mary?

（你有沒有聽到約翰和瑪麗的消息？）

B: No, what about them?

（沒有，他們怎麼了？）

A: They're going to have a baby.

（他們要生小孩了。）

B: Wow, that's great.

（哇，好棒。）

They've wanted one for a long time.

（他們一直希望有個小孩。）

A: I know.

（我知道。）

I'm really happy for them.

（我很替他們高興。）

B: Tell them congratulations if you see them.

（如果你看到他們，替我跟他們恭喜。）

More Practices:

A: I heard that Amy got into Harvard.

B: Yah, she's excited.

A: 我聽說艾米被哈佛大學錄取了。

B: 是的，她很興奮。

A: What was Jim so excited about?

B: His brother's getting married.

> **A:** 吉米為什麼那麼興奮？
>
> **B:** 他哥哥要結婚了。

A: Did you hear what happened to Mary?

B: Yah, she won a trip to Colorado.

> **A:** 你有沒有聽說瑪麗的事？
>
> **B:** 有啊，她贏了到科羅拉多旅行的票。

A: What's the big news?

B: We're having a baby?

> **A:** 有什麼大新聞？
>
> **B:** 我們要生小孩了。

單字

opera	[ˈɑpərə]	歌劇
kidding	[ˈkɪdɪŋ]	開玩笑
asleep	[əˈslip]	a. 睡著的
hockey	[ˈhɑkɪ]	曲棍球
really	[ˈriəlɪ]	真的
congratulations	[kən‚grætʃəˈleʃənz]	恭喜
excited	[ɪkˈsaɪtɪd]	感到興奮的
happen	[ˈhæpən]	發生
trip	[trɪp]	旅程；旅遊
news	[njuz]	新聞

Unit 10

最近的事件

MP3-11

Conversation 1:

A: How about that concert last night?

（昨晚的演唱會怎麼樣？）

B: Man, that was incredible.

（真是好棒。）

A: That was the first time I've been to a concert where they played all the songs I like.

（這是第一次我到一個演唱會，他們唱的全是我喜歡的歌。）

B: Yah, I was thinking the same thing.

（是啊，我也是這麼想。）

Conversation 2:

A: I can't believe that Jordan Scott won the election.

（我真不敢相信喬登史考特贏了選舉。）

B: I know.

（我知道。）

I couldn't believe it myself.

（我自己也不敢相信。）

A: I thought the news had made a mistake.

（我想新聞可能搞錯了。）

B: I'm really glad we've finally got someone in office who understands what it's like to be poor.

（我真高興，我們終於選了知道什麼叫做貧窮的人。）

A: No kidding.

（就是說嘛。）

B: Maybe he'll be able to pass some legislation that will help us out.

（或許他會制訂一些法律幫助我們。）

More Practices:

A: Did you watch the game last night?

B: Of course.

It was incredible.

A: 你有沒有看昨晚的比賽？

B: 當然有。

真是很棒。

A: I'm really sorry that your sister got hurt.

B: Thanks, I'm just glad that it's not too serious.

A: 我很難過你妹妹受了傷。

B: 謝謝你，我很高興還好傷得不嚴重。

A: Did you hear about the new grocery store that just opened up?

B: Yah, I went there yesterday.

Their prices are great!

A: 你有沒有聽說那一家新開張的雜貨店？

B: 聽說了，我昨天才去。

他們的價錢很好。

單字

concert	['kɑnsɚt]	n. 演奏會；音樂會
incredible	[ɪn'krɛdəbl̩]	（口語）很棒的
song	[sɔŋ]	歌
same	[sem]	相同的
election	[ɪ'lɛkʃən]	選舉
myself	[maɪ'sɛlf]	我自己
glad	[glæd]	高興；樂意
understand	[ˌʌndɚ'stænd]	瞭解；明白
pass	[pæs]	通過
legislation	[ˌlɛdʒɪs'leʃən]	立法
serious	['sɪrɪəs]	嚴重的
grocery store		雜貨店
price	[praɪs]	價格

家人

Conversation 1:

A: Is Mary coming home this weekend?
（瑪麗這個週末會回來嗎？）

B: She's supposed to.
（應該會。）

A: When will she be here?
（她什麼時候到？）

B: I think she said about 8 on Friday.
（我想她是說星期五八點。）

A: Why so late?
（為什麼那麼晚？）

B: She has class until 5.
（她的課上到五點。）

Conversation 2:

A: John, can you come here?
（約翰，你能過來嗎？）

B: Yah, what's going on?

（可以，什麼事？）

A: Do you think I should give Dad this tie or this one for his birthday?

（你認為我應該送給爸爸這條領帶還是這個做他的生日禮物？）

B: Hmm, he has a lot of black ones already.

（我已經有許多黑色的領帶了。）

A: That's true.

（那是真的。）

Do you think the red one will go with his suits?

（你想紅色會配他的西裝嗎？）

B: Yah, I think that one would be better.

（會，我認為那條會比較好。）

More Practices:

A: When's John coming home?

B: At 10.

    A: 約翰幾點會回來？

    B: 十點。

A: Does Dad work late tonight?

B: No, he gets off early.

A: 爸爸今晚會工作晚一點嗎？

B: 不，他會早一點回來。

A: Are you going to do any laundry today?

B: No, I think I'll wait until tomorrow.

A: 你今天要洗衣服嗎？

B: 不，我想我要等到明天再洗。

A: Can you give me a hand with these chores?

B: Yah, but I've only got a few minutes until I have to leave.

A: 你可以幫我這些雜務嗎？

B: 可以，但是我只有幾分鐘的時間，我有事要走。

單字

weekend	[ˈwikˈɛnd]	n. 週末
late	[let]	a. 很晚
until	[ʌnˈtɪl]	直到
tie	[taɪ]	領帶
birthday	[ˈbɝθˌde]	n. 生日
already	[ɔlˈrɛdɪ]	adv. 已經
suit	[sut]	西裝
better	[ˈbɛtɚ]	較好的；更好
early	[ˈɝlɪ]	早
chores	[tʃɔrz]	雜務

Chapter 4

社交英語

拜訪

Conversation 1:

A: What are you doing here?

（你在這裡做什麼？）

B: Oh, I just thought I'd drop by to say hi.

（噢，我只是想過來看看你。）

A: Well, that's nice of you.

（你真客氣。）

B: How have you been?

（你最近怎麼樣？）

A: Okay, but I've been better.

（還好，但是最近好多了。）

B: Oh, well maybe I can cheer you up a bit.

（或許我能讓你高興一點。）

More Practices:

A: Come in for a while.

B: Okay, we haven't talked in a while.

A: 進來做一下。

B: 好吧，我們好久沒聊天了。

A: Hey, Mary, do you mind if I come in?

B: No, that would be great.

    A: 嗨，瑪麗，我可以進來坐坐嗎？

    B: 可以，你來真好。

A: Steve's here.

    Do you feel like having company?

B: Sure, I'll be right there.

    A: 史帝夫在這裡。

        你要不要過來聊聊天？

    B: 好的，我馬上過去。

A: Hello John.

    I just dropped by to say hi.

B: Well, come on in.

    Do you want anything to drink?

    A: 哈囉，約翰。

        我只是過來坐坐。

    B: 進來吧。

        你要喝什麼飲料？

maybe	[′mebi]	也許
cheer	[tʃɪr]	（鼓勵）加油
mind	[maɪnd]	v. 介意
drink	[drɪŋk]	v. 喝（飲料）

13

介紹

Conversation 1:

A: Allow me to introduce myself.

（讓我來介紹我自己。）

I'm Tom.

（我叫湯姆。）

B: Nice to meet you, Tom.

（很高興認識你，湯姆。）

My name is Susan.

（我叫蘇珊。）

A: The pleasure is all mine.

（我很榮幸。）

B: You're so kind.

（你真好。）

Conversation 2:

A: John, this is my friend Austin.

（約翰，這是我的朋友奧斯汀。）

Austin, this is John.

（奧斯汀，這是約翰。）

B: Hi Austin.

（嗨，奧斯汀。）

C: Hi. Nice to meet you.

（嗨，很高興認識你。）

B: You too.

（我也很高興認識你。）

A: Austin went to high school with me.

（奧斯汀跟我上同一所高中。）

B: Oh, I've heard a lot of stories.

（噢，我常聽說你的事情。）

More Practices:

A: Mary, this is Kristina.

B: Hello.

A: 瑪麗，這是克麗絲婷娜。

B: 哈囉。

A: Mom, this is my friend John.

B: Hi John.

Nice to meet you.

A: 媽，這是我的朋友約翰。

B: 嗨，約翰。

很高興認識你。

A: John, I'd like you to meet my friend Tom.

B: Hello Tom.

A: 約翰，我跟你介紹我的朋友湯姆。

B: 哈囉，湯姆。

A: Robert, have you met Mary before?

B: No, I don't guess I have.

The pleasure is mine.

A: 羅伯，你以前見過瑪麗嗎？

B: 沒有，我不認為我們見過面。

很榮幸認識你。

單字

introduce	[ˌɪntrəˈdjus]	介紹
pleasure	[ˈplɛʒɚ]	榮幸
kind	[kaɪnd]	a. 良善
before	[bɪˈfor]	之前

邀約

Conversation 1:

A: Hello.

（哈囉。）

B: Mary, this is John.

（瑪麗，這是約翰。）

A: Hi, what's going on?

（嗨，有什麼事嗎？）

B: We got a couple of extra tickets to Les Miserables for tonight.

我們有多出兩張今晚『悲慘世界』的票。

We were wondering if you would like to go.

（你要不要去。）

A: Sure, that sounds fun.

（好啊，那可很好。）

B: Okay, just be ready about 7:30.

（好，七點半左右準備好。）

A: Are you doing anything this Friday?

（你星期五要做什麼事嗎？）

B: No, why?

（沒有，你為什麼問？）

A: I've got a couple of tickets to the hockey game.

（我有幾張曲棍球賽的票。）

Do you want to go?

（你要不要去？）

B: Are you kidding me?

（你開我玩笑嗎？）

A: No, I'm serious.

（沒有，我說真的。）

My friend couldn't use them so he gave them to me.

（我的朋友沒辦法去，所以把票給我。）

B: Man, that's awesome.

（哇，那真棒。）

I'll go.

（我去。）

I can even pay for parking if you want me to.

（你如果要我付停車費的話，我會付。）

A: Do you want to come over tonight?

B: Sure.

> A: 你今晚要過來嗎？
>
> B: 好的。

A: Do you feel like going to a movie?

B: No, I'd better just stay home and rest.

> A: 你要不要去看電影 ？
>
> B: 不要，我最好在家休息。

A: Mary, this is John.

I was wondering if you would like to go to the dance on Saturday.

B: I'm sorry, but I already have a date.

> A: 瑪麗，我是約翰。
>
> 我在想你星期六要不要去參加舞會。
>
> B: 對不起，但是我已經有伴一起去。

A: Wanna get something to eat?

B: Yah, let's go.

> A: 要不要去吃點東西？
>
> B: 好，走吧。

單字

couple	[ˈkʌpl̩]	n. 一對；一雙
extra	[ˈɛkstrə]	額外的；多餘的
ticket	[ˈtɪkɪt]	票
wonder	[ˈwʌndɚ]	想知道
ready	[ˈrɛdɪ]	準備好
game	[gem]	（球類）比賽
serious	[ˈsɪrɪəs]	認真的
awesome	[ˈɔsəm]	（口語）很棒的
parking	[ˈpɑrkɪŋ]	停車
stay	[ste]	停留
rest	[rɛst]	休息
Saturday	[ˈsætɚde]	星期六
already	[ɔlˈrɛdɪ]	adv. 已經
date	[det]	約會

在宴會或餐廳

MP3-16

Conversation 1:

A: Some party.

（真是不錯的宴會。）

B: Yah, this is fun.

（是啊，真好玩。）

A: Man, it's been like 10 years since I saw you.

（我上次看到你到現在已經十年了。）

B: I know.

（我知道。）

I feel like I'm in high school again.

（我覺得好像回到高中時期。）

A: So how've you been?

（你一向好嗎？）

B: Good.

（很好。）

I'm married and our oldest boy just started kindergarten.

（我結婚了，我最大的兒子剛上幼稚園。）

Conversation 2:

A: The waiter said we are going to be seated in just a minute.

（服務生說稍後就帶我們去就座。）

B: Good.

（很好。）

I'm hungry.

（我很餓。）

A: Have you ever eaten here before?

（你以前有沒有來這裡吃過飯？）

B: No, but I've heard that it's really good.

（沒有，但是我聽說很不錯。）

A: It is.

（是的。）

This is my favorite place.

（這是我最喜歡的餐廳。）

B: Great.

（真好。）

I'm glad we decided to have the meeting over dinner.

（我很高興我們決定一起吃晚餐。）

More Practices:

A: Are you enjoying the party?

B: Yes, thank you.

> A: 你玩得高興嗎？
>
> B: 很好，謝謝你。

A: It sure is nice to see everybody.

B: I love family get-togethers.

> A: 能看到大家真的很好。
>
> B: 我喜歡家庭聚會。

A: Are you coming to the party tomorrow too?

B: No, I think one party a weekend is enough for me.

> A: 明天的宴會你也會來嗎？
>
> B: 不，一個週末派對，對我來說已經夠了。

A: How's everything going?

B: Good.

This sure is a nice place.

　A: 一切還好嗎？

　B: 很好。

這個地方真好。

單字

fun	[fʌn]	好玩；樂趣
kindergarten	[ˈkɪndɚˌgɑrtn̩]	幼稚園
waiter	[ˈwetɚ]	侍者
hungry	[ˈhʌŋgrɪ]	餓
favorite	[ˈfevərɪt]	最喜歡的
place	[ples]	地方
decide	[dɪˈsaɪd]	v. 決定；判斷
enjoy	[ɪnˈdʒɔɪ]	享受；喜歡；感到樂趣
party	[ˈpɑrtɪ]	宴會；派對
enough	[ɪˈnʌf]	足夠的

Chapter 5

購物英語

16 在百貨公司問路

Conversation 1:

A: Can you tell me where the men's department is?
（請問男士部門在哪裡？）

B: Sure, it's on the second floor just by the elevator.
（男士部門就在二樓電梯旁。）

A: Thank you.
（謝謝你。）

B: You bet.
（不用客氣。）

Conversation 2:

A: Is the shoe department on this floor.
（鞋子部門是在這一樓嗎？）

B: No, it's on the third floor.
（不，鞋子部門在三樓。）

A: What's the easiest way to get there?
（到哪裡最簡單的方法是什麼？）

B: Just take that elevator to the third floor and it'll be on your left.

（搭電梯到三樓，鞋子部門就在你的左邊。）

A: Okay, thanks.

（好的，謝謝你。）

More Practices:

A: Where is the restroom?

B: It's in the corner of the store.

A: 洗手間在哪裡？

B: 在店裡的角落處。

A: Do you have a suit department?

B: Yes, it's just past the shoe department on your right.

A: 你們有沒有西裝部門？

B: 有，就在鞋子部門再過去，就在你的右邊。

A: Excuse me, can you tell me how to get to the Far East Department Store?

B: Sure, go to the south end of the mall and you can't miss it.

A: 對不起，請問如何到遠東百貨公司？

B: 你到大型購物中心的南端去，你就會看到。

A: Do you know where a toy store is?

B: Yah, go up here and turn right just past the food court.

A: 你知道玩具店在哪裡嗎？

B: 知道，從這裡走去，向右轉，就在小吃部旁邊。

單字

department	[dɪˈpɑrtmənt]	部門
second	[ˈsɛkənd]	第二
floor	[flor]	地板；樓層
elevator	[ˈɛləˌvetɚ]	電梯
third	[θɝd]	第三
way	[we]	方法
left	[lɛft]	左邊
restroom	[ˈrɛstrum]	洗手間
past	[pæst]	經過
mall	[mɔl]	大型購物中心
court	[kort]	球場

Conversation 1:

A: Can you give me a hand here?

（你可以幫我忙嗎？）

B: Sure, what do you need?

（好的，你需要什麼？）

A: Does this vacuum cleaner come with any attachments?

（這個吸塵器有沒有什麼附加物？）

B: No, this is the basic model.

（沒有，這是陽春型吸塵器。）

The next model up does come with attachments though.

（再往上一級的型號就有附件。）

A: How much more is it?

（差多少錢？）

B: It's about $20 more.

（多美金二十元。）

A: How long does this sale last?

（這次拍賣會有多久？）

B: Until the end of the month.

（直到月底。）

A: Do you think you'll still have any of these TV's then?

（你想你們仍然會有這些電視機嗎？）

B: Sure, we always have plenty.

（當然囉，我們總是有很多。）

More Practices:

A: How much is this toaster?

B: It's $14.95.

    A: 這個烤麵包機多少錢？

    B: 美金十四塊九毛五。

A: Does this TV come with a remote control?

B: It sure does.

    A: 這個電視機有遙控嗎？

    B: 有。

A: Do you have any calculators?

B: No, we're all out.

A: 你們有計算機嗎？

B: 沒有，賣完了。

單字

vacuum cleaner	[ˈvækjʊəm ˈklinɚ]	吸塵器
attachments	[əˈtætʃmənt]	附件
basic	[ˈbesɪk]	基本的
model	[ˈmɑdḷ]	機型
though	[ðo]	（口語）不過
sale	[sel]	拍賣
last	[læst]	v. 延續；持續
plenty	[ˈplɛntɪ]	很多
toaster	[ˈtostɚ]	烤麵包機
remote	[rɪˈmot]	n. 遙控器
control	[kənˈtrol]	控制
calculator	[ˈkælkjəˌletɚ]	計算機

付錢

MP3-19

Conversation 1:

A: That'll be $24.15.

（總共是美金二十四塊一毛五。）

B: Do you take credit card?

（你們收信用卡嗎？）

A: Sure.

（收。）

B: Okay, I'll pay it with credit card.

（好的，我用信用卡付。）

A: Okay, just sign here.

（好的，請在這裡簽名。）

Conversation 2:

A: Your total is $25.

（總共是美金二十五元。）

B: $25?

（二十五元？）

I thought this was on sale.

（不是在打折嗎？）

A: You're right.

（是了。）

I'm sorry.

（對不起。）

I'll fix it.

（我會改。）

B: No problem.

（好的。）

A: All right, the correct total is $17.

（好了，正確數目是十七塊錢。）

B: That sounds more like it.

（這還差不多。）

More Practices:

A: Your total is $10.

B: Okay, I'll pay with cash.

A: 總共是十塊錢。

B: 好的，我用現款付。

A: Do you take credit cards?

B: No, cash or check only.

> **A:** 你們收信用卡嗎？

> **B:** 沒有，只收現金或支票。

A: $11.84 is your total.

B: Here's a twenty.

> **A:** 總共是美金十一塊八毛四。

> **B:** 給你二十元。

A: $10.57 is your total.

Out of $20 $9.43 is your change.

B: Thanks.

> **A:** 總共是美金十元五毛七。

> 你給二十元，找你九塊四毛三。

> **B:** 謝謝。

單字

credit card		信用卡
sign	[saɪn]	簽名
total	[ˈtotl̩]	總共
fix	[fɪks]	修改
problem	[ˈprɑbləm]	問題
correct	[kəˈrɛkt]	adj. 正確的
cash	[kæʃ]	n. 現金

19

退錢

MP3-20

Conversation 1:

A: I'd like to return this sweater.

（我要退這件毛衣。）

B: Okay, do you have your receipt?

（好的，你有收據嗎？）

A: Yep.

（有。）

Here you go.

（在這裡。）

B: Do you want to exchange it for something else or get cash back?

（你要換其他東西還是要退錢？）

A: I'd like to have cash back.

（我要退錢。）

B: All right.

（好的。）

A: I need to return this TV.

（我要退這部電視。）

B: Is everything okay with the TV?

（這部電視沒問題吧？）

A: It works, but I'm just not too happy with it.

（沒有壞，但是我對它不滿意。）

I'd like to get a refund.

（我要退錢。）

B: Do you have your receipt?

（你有收據嗎？）

A: Yes, it's right here.

（有，在這裡。）

B: All right, we'll take care of this for you.

（好，我們會處理。）

More Practices:

A: I'd like to return this CD.

B: Okay, I can help you.

A: 我要退這個光碟。

B: 好的，我還幫你處理。

A: Can I help you?

B: Yes, this microwave is defective.

I'd like to get a refund.

A: 有什麼事嗎？

B: 是的，這個微波爐有瑕疵。

我要退錢。

A: I need to get a refund for this chair.

It's defective.

B: All right, Sally can help you in customer service.

A: 我要退這張椅子。

這張椅子有瑕疵。

B: 好的，顧客服務部的莎莉會幫你處理。

單字

return	[rɪ'tɝn]	退還
sweater	['swɛtɚ]	毛衣
receipt	[rɪ'sit]	收據
exchange	[ɪks'tʃendʒ]	交換
else	[ɛls]	其他的
cash	[kæʃ]	n. 現金
refund	[rɪ'fʌnd]	退款；退貨
microwave	['maɪkrə,wev]	微波爐
defective	[dɪ'fɛktɪv]	有缺陷的
customer	['kʌstəmɚ]	n. 顧客
service	['sɝvɪs]	服務

Chapter 6

餐廳英語

Unit

20 速食餐廳

MP3-21

Conversation 1:

A: Can I take your order?

（你要點什麼？）

B: I'll take a #3.

（我要三號套餐。）

A: What do you want to drink?

（你要什麼飲料？）

B: Coke.

（可樂。）

A: All right.

（好的。）

A #3 with a Coke.

（三號套餐，要可樂。）

That'll be $3.23.

（美金三塊兩毛三。）

A: Welcome to Wendy's.

（歡迎到『威帝餐廳』。）

B: I'll have a hot dog combo with Coke.

（我要熱狗和可樂。）

A: Do you want onions on your hot dog?

（你的熱狗要加洋蔥嗎？）

B: No thanks.

（不用，謝謝。）

A: Your total is $3.87.

（總共是三塊八毛七。）

B: Thanks.

（謝謝。）

More Practices:

A: May I take your order?

B: One moment please.

   A: 你要點菜了嗎？

   B: 請稍候。

A: I'll have a hamburger with no onions.

B: Would you like fries with that?

   A: 我要漢堡，不要放洋蔥。

B: 你要薯條嗎？

A: I'll have a large Coke.

B: 1 large Coke, do you want French fries?

A: 我要大杯可樂。

B: 一杯大杯可樂，要薯條嗎？

單字

order	[ˈɔrdɚ]	點菜
combo	[ˈkɑmbo]	套餐
onion	[ˈʌnjən]	洋蔥
hamburger	[ˈhæmbɝgɚ]	漢堡

Conversation 1:

A: Hello, how many do you have?

（哈囉，你們有幾個人？）

B: 4, for non-smoking.

（四個人，要不吸煙位子。）

A: Okay, there's about a 10 minute wait.

（好的，要等十分鐘。）

Can I have your name?

（你要什麼名字？）

B: Johnson.

（強生。）

A: I'll call you when it's ready.

（有位子時我會叫你。）

Conversation 2:

A: Hi, a table for two please.

（嗨，我要一張兩人的桌位。）

B: Smoking or non-smoking?

（抽煙區還是不吸煙區？）

A: Whatever's fastest.

（快一點的就好。）

B: Your name?

（你叫什麼名字？）

A: Mary.

（瑪麗。）

B: I'll call you when it's ready.

（一有桌位我就叫你。）

More Practices:

A: We'd like a table for two.

B: Right this way.

   A: 我要一張兩人的桌位。

   B: 這邊請。

A: Is there a wait for the smoking section?

B: No, you can seat yourself.

   A: 吸煙區要等嗎？

   B: 不用，你可以自行入座。

A: Table for 12.

B: Okay, it'll take a few minutes for us to get that ready.

> **A:** 我要一張十二人的桌位。
> **B:** 好的，要等一下，讓我們準備。

A: How many do you have?

B: Five.

> **A:** 你們有幾個人？
>
> **B:** 五位。

單字

smoking	[ˈsmokɪŋ]	抽煙；抽煙區
section	[ˈsɛkʃən]	區域
seat	[sit]	v. 就座
yourself	[jʊrˈsɛlf]	你自己

點菜

Conversation 1:

A: Are you ready to order?

（你可以點菜了嗎？）

B: Yes.

（可以。

I'll have the chicken sandwich.

（我要雞塊三明治。）

A: Fries or baked potato?

（你要薯條還是烤馬鈴薯？）

B: Baked potato.

（烤馬鈴薯。）

Conversation 2:

A: May I take your order?

（你可以點菜了嗎？）

B: I have a question.

（我有一個問題。）

How do you normally cook the prime rib?

（你們的大排骨通常都怎麼煮？）

A: Medium well, but we can cook it however you like.

（煮七、八分熟，但是，我們可以依你要煮多熟。）

B: Okay, I'll take the prime rib with a baked potato.

（好的，我要大排骨和烤馬鈴薯。）

Medium well sounds good.

（煮七、八分熟可以。）

A: No problem then.

（好。）

I'll have it out in a few minutes.

（我幾分鐘後就端出來。）

More Practices:

A: Are you ready to order?

B: No, I need a couple of minutes.

    A: 你可以點菜了嗎？

    B: 還沒，再等幾分鐘。

A: Are you ready to order?

B: Yes.

I want the shrimp and lobster.

A: 你可以點菜了嗎？

B: 可以。

我要蝦和龍蝦。

A: Have you decided?

B: No, we're still looking.

A: 你決定了嗎？

B: 還沒，我們還在看。

A: Should I give you a couple of minutes?

B: No, I'm ready.

I'll just have the chicken strips.

A: 你還要一些時間嗎？

B: 不需要，我已經可以點菜了。

我要雞條。

單字

chicken	[ˈtʃɪkɪn]	n. 雞
sandwich	[ˈsænwɪtʃ]	三明治
baked	[bekt]	烤的
question	[ˈkwɛstʃən]	n. 問題
normally	[ˈnɔrməlɪ]	通常；一般來說
shrimp	[ʃrɪmp]	蝦
lobster	[ˈlɑbstɚ]	龍蝦

其他的服務

Conversation 1:

A: Can I get you anything?

（你需要什麼東西嗎？）

B: Yah, I need a couple of napkins.

（是的，我需要紙巾。）

A: Anything else?

（還要什麼嗎？）

B: No, I guess that will do it.

（沒有了，我想這就行。）

A: I'll be right back.

（我馬上回來。）

B: Thanks.

（謝謝。）

Conversation 2:

A: Ma'am.

（小姐。）

B: Yes, what can I do for you?

（有什麼事嗎？）

A: Can I get a to-go box?

（請給我一個外賣盒子。）

B: Sure.

（好的。）

Do you want any dessert?

（你要什麼甜點嗎？）

A: No, I'm pretty full.

（不用，我已經很飽了。）

B: Okay, I'll be right back with your to-go box.

（好的，我馬上拿你的外賣盒子來。）

I'll also bring the check.

（我還會拿帳單過來。）

More Practices:

A: Can I get a couple of napkins?

B: Sure.

Here you go.

A: 請給我幾張紙巾。

B: 好的。

在這裡。

A: Do you need anything right now?

B: A little more dressing please.

> A: 你還需要什麼嗎？
>
> B: 再給我一些調味醬。

A: How is everything?

B: Good.

I could use a couple of rolls.

> A: 一切都還好嗎？
>
> B: 很好。
>
> 請給我一些小麵包。

A: Can I bring you anything else?

B: I guess we're ready for the check.

> A: 你還要什麼東西嗎？
>
> B: 我想我們可以結帳了。

單字

napkin	['næpkɪn]	餐巾；紙巾
dessert	[dɪ'zɝt]	n. （飯後）甜點
full	[fʊl]	吃飽；滿的
dressing	['drɛsɪŋ]	（沙拉）調味醬
check	[tʃɛk]	n. 帳單

Chapter 7

校園英語

上課

MP3-25

Conversation 1:

A: What are you taking this semester?
（你這學期修什麼課？）

B: Biology, French, and English.
（生物，法文和英文。）

A: Are your classes tough?
（你的課難嗎？）

B: No, it's actually pretty easy.
（不難，事實上蠻輕鬆的。）

A: That's great.
（那很好。）

B: Yah, it's nice to have an easy semester.
（很好，能有一學期輕鬆是好的。）

Conversation 2:

A: How many hours are you taking?
（你修幾小時的課？）

B: 15.

（十五小時。）

A: That's a lot.

（那很多。）

B: Yah, but it's not too bad.

（是，但是還好。）

A: Do you like your classes?

（你喜歡你修的課嗎？）

B: Oh yah, they're all great.

（噢，喜歡，都很棒。）

More Practices:

A: What are you taking this semester?

B: Just English and History.

A: 你這學期修什麼課？
B: 就是英文和歷史。

A: How many classes are you taking?

B: 5, but they're all pretty good.

A: 你修幾門課？
B: 五科，但是，每科都很棒。

A: What's your toughest class this semester?

B: I don't know.

I guess they're all about the same.

A: 這學起你哪一門課最難？

B: 我不知道。

我想都差不多。

單字

semester	[sə'mɛstɚ]	學期
biology	[baɪ'ɑlədʒɪ]	n. 生物學
French	[frɛntʃ]	法語；法文
English	['ɪŋglɪʃ]	英語
tough	[tʌf]	（口語）艱難
actually	['æktʃʊəlɪ]	adv. 實際上；事實上
History	['hɪstrɪ]	歷史

老師

MP3-26

Conversation 1:

A: Who do you have for History?

（你的歷史課是哪一位老師？）

B: Dr. Smith.

（史密斯博士。）

A: Is he new?

（是新來的嗎？）

B: No, he's been here for a while.

（不是，他在這裡好一陣子了。）

A: That's weird, I've never heard of him.

（那真奇怪，我從沒聽過。）

B: Well, he only teaches one class.

（他只教一門課。）

Conversation 2:

A: How do you like Dr. Scott?

（你喜歡史考特博士嗎？）

B: He's great.

（他很棒。）

A: No kidding.

（就是啊。）

He really knows his stuff.

（他對他教的東西很懂。）

B: Yah, I think he's in the running for teacher of the year.

（是的，我想他被提名競選年度最佳老師。）

A: Wow, that would be cool.

（哇，那真棒。）

More Practices:

A: Who do you have for Algebra?

B: Mrs. White.

A: 你的代數課誰教？

B: 懷特老師。

A: Who teaches that class?

B: Dr. Jones.

A: 誰教那門課？

B: 瓊斯博士。

A: Is your History professor any good?

B: No, she's not that good.

> **A:** 你的歷史教授好嗎？
>
> **B:** 不好，她不那麼好。

A: What do you think of Dr. Lewis?

B: I don't know.

I haven't figured her out yet.

> **A:** 你認為路易斯博士怎麼樣？
>
> **B:** 我不知道。
>
> 我對她不太清楚。

單字

weird	[wɪrd]	奇怪的
stuff	[stʌf]	n. 東西；材料
Algebra	[ˈældʒəbrə]	代數
professor	[prəˈfɛsɚ]	教授
figure	[ˈfɪgjɚ]	（口語）明白；理解
yet	[jɛt]	adv. 尚未

Conversation 1:

A: What did you think of that test?

（那個考試你覺得怎麼樣？）

B: I thought it was easy.

（我認為很簡單。）

A: Are you serious?

（你說真的？）

B: Yah, what did you think?

（是啊，你認為呢？）

A: I thought it was terrible, but I didn't really study.

（我認為很糟，但是我沒有認真念。）

B: Well, what do you expect?

（那，你還期待什麼？）

Conversation 2:

A: How was your test?

（你考試考得如何？）

B: It was all right.

（還好。）

A: Do you think you did well?

（你想你考得好嗎？）

B: I don't know.

（我不知道。）

There were some questions that I didn't really expect.

（有一些題目，我沒有想到會考。）

A: I hate that.

（我最討厭這種事。）

B: Yah, I guess I'll find out soon enough.

（是啊，我想我很快就會知道。）

More Practices:

A: What did you think of the test?

B: It was easy.

    A: 你認為這次考試怎麼樣？

    B: 很簡單。

A: How was the test?

B: All right.

I think I made a B.

A: 你考得怎樣？

B: 還好。

我想我會拿個 B。

A: Did you get the answer to the third question?

B: No, I have no idea what that one was about.

A: 第三題你知道答案嗎？

B: 不知道，那一題我不知道在說什麼。

A: How do you think you did on the test?

B: Great.

I don't think I missed anything.

A: 你認為你考得怎麼樣？

B: 很好。

我不認為我有做錯哪一題。

單字

test	[tɛst]	測驗；考試
really	[ˈriəlɪ]	真的
terrible	[ˈtɛrəbl̩]	（口語）糟透的
expect	[ɪkˈspɛkt]	預期；期待
hate	[het]	恨；不喜歡
answer	[ˈænsɚ]	答案；回答
third	[θɝd]	第三
miss	[mɪs]	v. 做錯

室友

MP3-28

Conversation 1:

A: Have you found out who your roommate is yet?

（你知道誰是你的室友嗎？）

B: Yes, you're not going to believe this.

（知道，你絕不會相信。）

It's Sally Smith.

（是莎莉史密斯。）

A: Are you serious?

（真的？）

B: Yes.

（是啊。）

A: I thought you told the director that you didn't want to live with her.

（我以為你跟主任說過，你不要跟她一起住。）

B: I did.

（我說過了。）

I guess she wrote it down wrong or something.

（我想她寫錯了，或是其他什麼原因。）

Conversation 2:

A: How do you like your roommate?

（你喜歡你的室友嗎？）

B: He's pretty cool.

（他很棒。）

Do you want to meet him?

（你要見他嗎？）

A: Sure.

（好啊。）

B: We're going to the movies later.

（我們稍後要一起去看電影。）

Why don't you come with us?

（你要不要一起來？）

A: Okay.

（好。）

B: Good, I think you'll like him.

（好，我想你會喜歡他。）

A: Who's the new roommate?

B: Her name is Mary.

    A: 那位新來的室友是誰？

    B: 她的名字叫瑪麗。

A: How's it going with your new roommate?

B: Not too good.

We're just too different.

    A: 你跟你的新室友處得如何？

    B: 還好。

我們只是很不相同。

A: Do you like your new roommate?

B: I haven't met him yet.

    A: 你喜歡你的新室友嗎？

    B: 我還沒遇見他。

單字

roommate	[ˈrumˌmet]	室友
director	[dəˈrɛktɚ]	主任
wrong	[rɔŋ]	錯誤的；出錯
different	[ˈdɪfərənt]	a. 不同的

Chapter 8

度假

28

計畫旅遊

MP3-29

Conversation 1:

A: What time do you want to leave for the vacation?

（你們打算什麼時候要離開去度假？）

B: I thought we could leave about 8 in the morning.

（我想我們會在早上八點左右離開。）

A: That would be good.

（那很好。）

We could stop for lunch at noon.

（我們可以在中午停下來吃午餐。）

B: Yah, that way we could get there by about 3.

（好，那樣我們可以在三點左右到那裡。）

A: Good.

（好。）

I'm glad we got that settled.

（我很高興一切説定了。）

A: Where do you want to go once we're in San Antonio?

（我們到了聖安東尼之後你要去哪裡？）

B: I heard the River Walk is cool.

（我聽說河邊漫步道很棒。）

A: Yah, then we could go by the mall.

（是啊，然後我們可以到大型購物中心去。）

B: What time do you want to get there?

（你什麼時候要去？）

A: I don't know.

（我不知道。）

Maybe around noon.

（可能中午左右。）

B: Okay.

（好的。）

More Practices:

A: What time should we leave for the airport?

B: 7:30.

A: 我們什麼時候該去機場？

B: 七點半。

A: Where do we pick up the rental car?

B: The airport.

    A: 我們在哪裡拿租車？

    B: 在機場。

A: What time should we schedule the flight?

B: As late as possible.

    A: 我們的班機應該排在什麼時候？

    B: 盡量晚一點。

A: Where should we go first on the trip?

B: I always like to get to the hotel.

    A: 我們首先應該去哪裡？

    B: 我總是喜歡先到旅館。

單字

vacation	[vəˈkeʃən]	n. 休假；假期
leave	[liv]	離開
settle	[ˈsɛtl̩]	安頓
around	[əˈraʊnd]	（時間）前後；大約
airport	[ˈɛrˌport]	n. 飛機場
rental	[ˈrɛntl̩]	出租
schedule	[ˈskɛdʒʊl]	v. 安排（時間）
flight	[flaɪt]	飛行；班機
hotel	[hoˈtɛl]	旅館；飯店

上飛機

Conversation 1:

A: They're about to start boarding for the flight.

（他們正要開始登機。）

B: Do we get to go first?

（我們可以先上去嗎？）

A: No, they call them by seat numbers.

（不行，他們是按照座位號碼叫人。）

We'll probably be last.

（我們可能是最後登機。）

B: Okay, I'm going to get a paper then.

（好的，那我要去買份報紙。）

A: All right, but be quick.

（好的，但是要快點。）

Conversation 2:

A: Boarding for flight 403 to New York will start in five minutes.

（到紐約的 403 號班機五分鐘內登機。）

B: That's our flight.

（那是我們的班機。）

C: Good, I'm ready to get out of here.

（好的，我已經準備好要離開這裡。）

B: You're not worried about flying?

（你不擔心飛行嗎？）

C: No, it's safer than driving.

（不擔心，比開車安全。）

B: That's true.

（那是真的。）

More Practices:

A: Flight 657 to Hong Kong is boarding now.

B: Oh, that's me.

I've got to go.

A: 往香港的 657 號班機現在開始登機。

B: 噢，那是我的班機。

我該走了。

A: Is your flight boarding yet?

B: Yes, but I've got a couple of minutes.

A: 你的班機在登機了嗎？

B: 是的，但是我還有幾分鐘。

A: When does first class board?

B: I think we get to go on first.

A: 頭等艙什麼時候登機？

B: 我想我們可以先登機。

A: Do you get to board first if you arrive here earlier?

B: Not really, they do it all by seat numbers.

A: 如果你早到可以先登機嗎？

B: 不行，他們是按照座位號碼登機。

單字

boarding	[ˈbordɪŋ]	登機（board 的現在分詞）
first	[fɝst]	首先
last	[læst]	最後的
quick	[kwɪk]	a. 快的
worried	[ˈwɝɪd]	憂心；擔心
flying	[ˈflaɪɪŋ]	飛行
first class		頭等艙
earlier	[ˈɝlɪɚ]	a. 稍早；較早的

目的地的天氣

MP3-31

Conversation 1:

A: I wonder what the weather is like in Chicago.

（我不知道芝加哥天氣是如何？）

B: Probably cold.

（可能很冷。）

A: I know that, but I wonder if it's snowing.

（我知道，但是我不知道是否在下雪。）

B: Ask the attendant.

（問空服員。）

She should know.

（她應該知道。）

A: That's not a bad idea.

（那是個好主意。）

Conversation 2:

A: Have you heard what the weather is like in New York?

（你有沒有聽說紐約的天氣如何？）

114

B: Yah, it's clear today.

（聽説了，今天是晴天。）

It should be cloudy and rainy most of tomorrow though.

（明天應該會多雲而且下雨。）

A: Man, I wish it would stay clear.

（我真希望能繼續是晴天。）

This may be the only time I ever go to New York.

（這次可能是我到紐約唯一的一次。）

B: Well, I guess we'll find out tomorrow.

（我想我們明天就會知道。）

More Practices:

A: Is it raining in Dallas?

B: No, it's clear.

A: 達拉斯在下雨嗎？

B: 不，是晴天。

A: Has the pilot said what the weather's like at the other airport?

B: No, but I think he's about to.

A: 飛行員有沒有説另一個機場的氣候如何？

B: 還沒，但是我想他就要説了。

A: What did they say about the weather in Seattle?

B: Raining, of course.

> **A:** 他們說西雅圖的天氣怎麼樣？
> **B:** 當然是在下雨。

A: Will the rain delay our landing?

B: Maybe, it just depends how bad it is when we get there.

> **A:** 下雨會讓我們的降落延遲嗎？
> **B:** 或許會，完全是看我們到達的時候有多糟。

單字

wonder	[′wʌndɚ]	想；想知道
weather	[′wɛðɚ]	天氣
snow	[sno]	下雪
attendant	[ə′tɛndənt]	n. 服務人員
idea	[aɪ′dɪə]	主意
clear	[klɪr]	晴朗
delay	[dɪ′le]	v. n. 延遲
landing	[lændɪŋ]	v. 著陸（land 的現在分詞）
depend	[dɪ′pɛnd]	v. 視～而定

31

觀光

Conversation 1:

A: Do you want to do some sightseeing?

（你要去觀光嗎？）

B: Sure.

（好的。）

Where do you want to go first?

（你想先去哪裡？）

A: How about the White House?

（要去白宮嗎？）

B: That sounds good.

（好啊。）

A: I'll be waiting in the car.

（我在車上等著。）

Conversation 2:

A: What time does our tour leave?

（我們的團什麼時候離開？）

B: At 10.

（十點。）

A: I don't remember if they said to bring lunch or not.

（我不記得他們有沒有說要帶午餐。）

B: I'm not sure, but I bet they provide lunch.

（我不太確定，但是我想他們應該有供應午餐。）

A: Maybe I should call.

（或許我應該打電話問看看。）

B: Yah, better safe than sorry.

（是，那是比較保險的作法。）

More Practices:

A: I'd like to go on the 4 o' clock tour.

B: I'm sorry, it's already full

    A: 我想參加四點的團。

    B: 對不起，但是那一團已經滿額了。

A: How much is the Island Tour?

B: It's $25.

    A: 島嶼參觀多少錢？

    B: 美金二十五元。

A: When does the Ski Tour leave today?

B: In one hour.

    A: 滑雪團什麼時候離開？

    B: 一小時內。

單字

sightseeing	[ˈsaɪtˌsiɪŋ]	觀光
tour	[tʊr]	旅遊
remember	[rɪˈmɛmbɚ]	記得
provide	[prəˈvaɪd]	v. 準備；供給
safe	[sef]	a. 安全的

Chapter 9

請假

Conversation 1:

A: I don't feel very well.

（我不是很舒服。）

B: I know.

（我知道。）

I heard you throwing up.

（我聽到你在吐。）

You should stay home.

（你應該留在家裡。）

A: Okay, will you call John and tell him I'm not coming in?

（好的，你可以打電話給約翰，告訴他我不能來嗎？）

B: Yah, why don't you go back to bed and get some rest.

（好的，你何不回到床上去休息。）

A: How many sick days do you have with your job?

（你上班的地方可以有幾天病假？）

B: 10, but I also have 5 personal days.

（十天，但是我也有五天事假。）

A: Do your sick days roll over if you don't use them all?

（如果你的病假沒有用完，可以到隔年用嗎？）

B: No, they stopped doing that a year ago.

（不行，他們一年前取消這麼做。）

More Practices:

A: Will you call in and tell them I'm sick?

B: Sure.

A: 你可以打個電話告訴他們我病了嗎？

B: 好的。

A: John, this is Mary.

I'm not going to make it in today.

I'm a little bit under the weather.

B: Okay, I hope you get to feeling better.

A: 約翰，我是瑪麗。

我今天不能來。

B: 好的，我希望你能好一點。

A: I feel awful.

I don't think they could drag me to work today.

B: I'll call them for you.

A: 我覺得很不舒服。

我不認為他們可以拉我去上班。

B: 我替你打電話給他們。

A: Did you sleep last night?

B: No, I kept waking up and having to go to the bathroom all night.

I called work and told them I was sick.

A: 你昨晚有沒有睡？

B: 沒有，我一直醒來，整晚去上好幾趟廁所。

我已經打電話給公司，跟他們說我病了。

單字

throw up		（口語）嘔吐
rest	[rɛst]	休息
sick	[sɪk]	生病；不舒服
personal	[ˈpɜsn̩l]	私人的
awful	[ˈɔful]	a. 很糟的
drag	[dræg]	拖
bathroom	[ˈbæθˌrum]	浴室；廁所

要去看醫生

MP3-34

Conversation 1:

A: I'm not going to come in this Friday.

（星期五我不能來。）

I have a doctor's appointment.

（我要去看醫生。）

B: Is something wrong?

（有什麼問題嗎？）

A: I hope not.

（我希望沒有。）

It's just a regular check-up.

（只是例行身體檢查。）

B: Oh, I hope everything turns out all right.

（噢，我希望一切都沒問題。）

A: Me too.

（我也是。）

A: I'll be a little late tomorrow.

（我明天會晚一點才來。）

I have a doctor's appointment at 10.

（我十點要去看醫生。）

B: Are you all right?

（你沒問題吧？）

A: I don't know.

（我不知道。）

I found a lump the other day.

（前幾天我發現一個硬塊。）

I wanted to make sure I got it checked out.

（我想要確實檢查一下。）

B: Definitely.

（那當然囉。）

More Practices:

A: I'm not going to make it in tomorrow.

I have a doctor's appointment.

B: Okay.

　　A: 我明天不能來。

我要去看醫生。

B: 好的。

A: I'm going to see the doctor Thursday.

I guess I'll have to take a sick day.

B: No problem.

A: 星期四我要去看醫生。

我想我得請病假。

B: 沒問題。

A: I got a note that said you aren't going to be here next Wednesday.

Is that right?

B: Yes, I'm going to see the doctor.

A: 我接到字條說你下星期三不能來。

是真的嗎？

B: 是的，我要去看醫生。

A: You look pretty bad.

You need to see a doctor.

B: I know.

I'm going in tomorrow.

That's why I won't be here tomorrow.

A: 你看起來精神很不好。

你應該去看醫生。

B: 我知道。

我明天要去。

所以我明天不能來。

單字

appointment	[ə'pɔɪntmənt]	約定時間
regular	['rɛgjələ˞]	普通的
check-up	['tʃɛk͵ʌp]	檢查
lump	[lʌmp]	硬塊
definitely	['dɛfənətlɪ]	當然

事假

Conversation 1:

A: I'm not going to be here Friday.

（我星期五不能來。）

B: How come?

（為什麼？）

A: I'm taking a personal day.

（我要請事假。）

My aunt is coming in from New York.

（我姨媽從紐約來。）

B: That sounds like fun.

（聽起來是件高興的事。）

A: I haven't seen her in about three years.

（我大約三年沒見過她。）

B: I hope you have a good time.

（我希望你們愉快。）

A: This week has been so busy.

（這個星期真忙。）

B: I know.

（我知道。）

I need a break.

（我需要休息一下。）

A: I'm going to take a personal day as soon as all this stuff is over.

（等這些事情一過，我就要請事假。）

B: That's not a bad idea.

（聽起來是個好主意。）

A: Yah, I've still got all 5 for the year.

（是的，我今年還有五天假期可以請。）

I might as well use them.

（我不如把假期用完。）

B: Exactly.

（確實。）

More Practices:

A: We've got a meeting this Friday at 11.

You can be there, right?

B: No, I'm taking a Personal Day Friday.

> **A:** 這個星期五,十一點有個會議。
>
> 你可以來吧?
>
> **B:** 不行,我星期五要請事假。

A: Why are you taking a personal day tomorrow?

B: Well, funny as it sounds, it is pretty personal.

I'd rather not go into details.

> **A:** 你明天為什麼要請事假?
>
> **B:** 聽起來很好笑,但那是私事。
>
> 我不想告訴你細節。

A: Mary, how many personal days do I have left this year?

B: I'm not sure.

I'll have to check the records and get back with you.

> **A:** 瑪麗,我今年還有幾天事假可以請?
>
> **B:** 我不知道。
>
> 我得查記錄,然後再跟你説。

A: I'm going to take a personal day tomorrow.

My daughter is coming in from San Francisco.

B: Okay, have a good time.

A: 我明天要請事假。

我女兒從三藩市來看我。

B: 好的，希望你愉快。

單字

personal	[ˈpɝsn̩l]	私人的
aunt	[ænt]	n. 姨媽
busy	[ˈbɪzɪ]	忙的
break	[brek]	n. 短暫的休息
stuff	[stʌf]	n. 事情
over	[ˈovɚ]	a. 結束
exactly	[ɪgˈzæktlɪ]	確實
funny	[ˈfʌnɪ]	好笑得

Unit

35

休假

MP3-36

Conversation 1:

A: I'm really glad that we get three weeks of paid vacation.

（我很高興，我們有三個星期的假期。）

B: Me too.

（我也是。）

I just wish I could go on trips for three weeks.

（我只希望我能夠去旅遊三星期。）

A: Why don't you?

（你何不去？）

B: It gets pretty expensive, you know.

（旅遊很貴的。）

A: So what do you do on vacation?

（那你假日做什麼？）

B: We take one trip a year, but the rest of the time we just take it easy and goof off.

（我們一年去旅遊一次，其他的時間就是放輕鬆，偷懶一下。）

A: John, I'm going to take my vacation next month.

（約翰，我下個月要休假。）

B: Do you have a date picked out?

（你選好哪一天了嗎？）

A: No, I wanted to ask you what a good time might be.

（還沒，我想問你哪一天比較好。）

B: It would be better if you could go near the beginning of the month, but it's really up to you.

（我較希望你能在月初請假，但是我是隨便你。）

A: Okay, I just wanted to make sure that I asked you.

（好的，我只是要跟你確定一下。）

More Practices:

A: Does your job offer paid vacations?

B: No, not until I've been there a little bit longer.

　　A: 你們公司給你假期嗎？

　　B: 沒有，要做久一點才有。

A: How much vacation time do you get?

B: None.

Can you believe that?

> **A:** 你一年可以休假多久？
>
> **B:** 沒休假。
>
> 真是令人難以置信。

A: When are you taking your vacation?

B: Sometime in the summer.

> **A:** 你什麼時候休假？
>
> **B:** 在夏天挑個時候。

A: Do you get to pick when you take your vacation?

B: Oh yah.

> **A:** 你可以選擇什麼時候休假嗎？
>
> **B:** 噢，可以。

單字

vacation	[vəˈkeʃən]	n. 休假；假期
paid	[ped]	有付錢的
expensive	[ɪkˈspɛnsɪv]	昂貴的
goof off		隨便混
date	[det]	日期
near	[nɪr]	靠近
offer	[ˈɔfɚ]	V. 提供

Chapter 10

娛樂英語

音樂

MP3-37

Conversation 1:

A: Do you like country music?

（你喜歡鄉村音樂嗎？）

B: No, I can't stand it.

（不，我受不了。）

I listen to classical music.

（我聽古典音樂。）

A: I never thought of you as someone who liked all that high class stuff.

（我沒想到你是那種喜歡那種高格調東西的人。）

B: Well, it's pretty relaxing when I've had a tough day.

（如果我一天很累了，古典音樂蠻令人輕鬆的。）

A: I can see that.

（我看得出來。）

A: What kind of music do you like?

（你喜歡什麼音樂？）

B: I listen to all kinds of music, but I think I like Contemporary Christian the best.

（我什麼音樂都聽，但是我最喜歡現代的基督教音樂。）

A: Is it any good?

（好聽嗎？）

B: You'd be surprised.

（你會異想不到。）

There are a lot of great Christian artists out there.

（市面上有很多很好的基督教音樂家。）

A: I'll have to check it out.

（我得聽聽看。）

B: Yah, you really ought to.

（是，你應該聽。）

More Practices:

A: What sort of music do you listen to?

B: Mostly rock and roll.

A: 你聽什麼音樂？

B: 大部分是搖滾樂。

A: Do you play any instruments?

B: I play the guitar a little bit.

    A: 你彈什麼樂器嗎？

    B: 我會彈一點吉他。

A: What do you do for fun?

B: I play the piano a lot.

    A: 你平常做什麼消遣？

    B: 我常彈鋼琴。

單字

country	[ˈkʌntrɪ]	a. 鄉村的
music	[ˈmjuzɪk]	音樂
stand	[stænd]	v. 忍受
classical	[ˈklæsɪkl]	古典的
listen	[ˈlɪsn]	v. 聽
stuff	[stʌf]	n. 東西
relaxing	[rɪˈlæksɪŋ]	a. 放輕鬆
tough	[tʌf]	（口語）艱難
kind	[kaɪnd]	種類
surprised	[sɚˈpraɪzd]	訝異的；驚訝的
sort	[sɔrt]	種類
instrument	[ˈɪnstrəmənt]	樂器
guitar	[gɪˈtɑr]	吉他
piano	[pɪˈæno]	鋼琴

看電影

MP3-38

Conversation 1:

A: Have you been to a movie recently?

（你最近有去看電影嗎？）

B: No, I hardly ever go.

（沒有，我幾乎不看電影。）

A: That's weird, you used to go all the time.

（那就奇怪了，你以前常看電影的。）

B: I know, I guess I just got tired of it.

（我知道，我想我是看煩了。）

A: Well, you still ought to see the new Star Wars film.

（你還是應該去看新的星際大戰。）

It's pretty good.

（拍得很好。）

B: Yah, I probably will.

（是啊，我或許應該去看。）

Conversation 2:

A: Do you want to catch a movie?

（要不要去看電影？）

B: Sure, what's playing?

（好啊，在演什麼？）

A: The Wizard of Oz is back in theaters.

（綠野仙蹤又重新來上演。）

B: Yah, I heard they fixed it up.

（是啊，我聽說影片整修過。）

A: That's what I heard too.

（我也這麼聽說。）

I think it should be good.

（我想應該會很好看。）

More Practices:

A: What's playing at the movies?

B: The Lord of the Rings is out.

　　A: 戲院在上演什麼？

　　B: 魔戒首部曲。

A: How often do you catch a flick?

B: Two or three times a month.

    A: 你多久看一次電影？

    B: 一個月兩、三次。

A: What do you do when you're bored?

B: I go to a lot of movies.

    A: 你無聊的時候都做什麼？
    B: 我常看電影。

A: Have you seen A Beautiful Mind yet?

B: No, but I heard it's supposed to be good.

    A: 你看過『美麗境界』沒有？

    B: 沒有，但是我聽說應該很好看。

單字

recently	[ˈrisn̩tlɪ]	最近地
hardly	[ˈhɑrdlɪ]	幾乎不
weird	[wɪrd]	奇怪的
film	[fɪlm]	電影
theater	[ˈθiətɚ]	戲院
flick	[flɪk]	（口語）電影
bored	[bord]	無聊的

電視

Conversation 1:

A: What do you watch on TV?

（你都看什麼電視節目？）

B: Not much anymore.

（我很少看電視。）

All the good shows are gone.

（所有好的節目都不見了。）

A: Tell me about it.

（就是說嘛！）

Once X-file went off the air there hasn't been much.

（『X 檔案』不演後，就沒什麼好看的了。）

B: I still like Friends though.

（我還是喜歡看『朋友』。）

A: Yah, it's pretty good.

（是啊，那個影集不錯。）

A: What channel is CNN?

B: 24.

> **A:** CNN 在第幾個頻道？
>
> **B:** 24。

A: Is there a game on today?

B: Yah, the Cowboy play at 7:30 on channel 10.

> **A:** 今晚有球賽轉播嗎？
>
> **B:** 有，『牛仔隊』七點半要打球，在第十頻道。

A: What's on TV tonight?

B: Not much of anything.

> **A:** 今晚電視上有什麼節目？
>
> **B:** 沒什麼好看的。

A: Do you want to come over and watch some TV?

B: Sure, I was going to watch it anyway.

> **A:** 你要不要過來看電視？
> **B:** 好，我反正要看。

單字

show	[ʃo]	節目
air	[ɛr]	（電視的）廣播
channel	[ˈtʃænl̩]	n. （電視）頻道
anyway	[ˈɛnɪˌwe]	無論如何

看書

MP3-40

Conversation 1:

A: Do you read a lot?

（你常看書嗎？）

B: All the time.

（總是在看書。）

A: Wow, I can't even finish one book.

（哇，我連一本書也看不完。）

B: I used to be like that, but I just got into reading.

（我以前也是那樣，但是現在看書成了我的消遣。）

Conversation 2:

A: What kind of books do you read?

（你看什麼書？）

B: I read a lot of mysteries.

（我看很多懸疑小說。）

What about you?

（你呢？）

A: I read a lot of biographies.

（我看很多自傳。）

B: Hmm, I don't know that I've ever read a biography.

（我不知道我有沒有看過自傳。）

A: I like them.

（我喜歡自傳。）

It's really amazing what has happened to some people.

（有些人的經歷真的很有趣。）

B: That's true.

（那是真的。）

More Practices:

A: Where do you go to get books?

B: If I don't go to the library, I go to bookstores.

> **A:** 你到哪裡去拿那些書？
> **B:** 如果我不去圖書館，我就去書店。

A: What kind of books do you read?

B: Mostly war books.

> **A:** 你讀什麼書？
> **B:** 大部分是戰爭的書。

A: Do you read much?

B: Yah, I read two or three books a month.

> **A:** 你常看書嗎？
> **B:** 是，我一個月看兩三本。

A: Do you like to read?

B: I love it.

It's so much fun.

> **A:** 你喜歡看書嗎？
> **B:** 喜歡。
>
> 看書很有趣。

單字

finish	[ˈfɪnɪʃ]	完成
mystery	[ˈmɪstərɪ]	n. 懸疑
biography	[baɪˈɑgrəfɪ]	自傳
amazing	[əˈmezɪŋ]	a. 令人驚嘆的
library	[ˈlaɪˌbrɛrɪ]	n. 圖書館
bookstore	[ˈbʊkˌstor]	書店
mostly	[ˈmostlɪ]	多半
war	[wɔr]	n. 戰爭

其他娛樂

Conversation 1:

A: What do you do when you have free time?

（你有空的時候都做什麼？）

B: I like to go shopping.

（我喜歡去逛街。）

A: I bet that gets expensive.

（我想那會很貴。）

B: Not really.

（不會。）

I don't buy much.

（我不買什麼東西。）

A: Are you serious?

（真的？）

B: Yah, I know it sound weird.

（是啊，聽起來很奇怪。）

A: What do you do with your free time?

（你有空的時候做什麼？）

B: I like to go down to the homeless shelter and help out.

（我喜歡去流浪漢收容所幫忙。）

A: That's really nice.

那真好。

Do they need others to help?

（他們需要其他幫手嗎？）

B: Sure, they could always use some extra help.

（當然，他們隨時需要更多的幫手。）

A: I think I'll go with you sometime then.

（我想，我有時會跟你一起去。）

More Practices:

A: Do you have any free time this week?

B: Yah, I think I'm going to play some golf.

　　A: 你這星期有空嗎？

　　B: 有，我想我會去打高爾夫球。

A: Do you have any hobbies?

B: I collect stamps.

> **A:** 你有什麼嗜好？
> **B:** 我集郵。

A: What do you do in your free time?

B: I like to get out in the woods and just watch the animals.

> **A:** 你有空做什麼？
>
> **B:** 我喜歡到樹林去，看動物。

單字

free	[fri]	a. 有空的
expensive	[ɪk'spɛnsɪv]	昂貴的
homeless	['homlɪs]	無家可歸的
shelter	['ʃɛltɚ]	n. 收容所
extra	['ɛkstrə]	額外的；多餘的
golf	[gɔlf]	打高爾夫球
hobby	['hɑbɪ]	嗜好
collect	[kə'lɛkt]	v. 收集
stamp	[stæmp]	郵票
woods	[wʊdz]	森林
animal	['ænəml̩]	動物

Chapter 11

生病的英語

頭痛

MP3-42

Conversation 1:

A: My head is killing me.

（我的頭好痛。）

B: Have you taken anything?

（你有沒有吃什麼藥？）

A: Yes, but it's not helping.

（有，但是沒有用。）

B: Try rubbing your head.

（試著揉揉你的頭。）

Sometimes that helps.

（有時候有效。）

A: Yah, I've heard of that.

（是，我聽說過。）

B: It helps me out.

（那對我有效。）

More Practices:

A: What do you take for a headache?

B: Tylenol.

> **A:** 你頭痛吃什麼藥？
>
> **B:** Tylenol.（止痛藥）

A: Do you get headaches that often?

B: All the time.

> **A:** 你常常頭痛嗎？
> **B:** 常常痛。

A: What do you do when you have a headache?

B: I usually sit down and try to relax.

> **A:** 你頭痛的時候怎麼辦？
>
> **B:** 我通常坐下來，試著放輕鬆。

A: Do you have any medicine for a headache?

B: Sure, take some Alleve.

> **A:** 你有什麼藥治頭痛嗎？
>
> **B:** 有，吃一些 Alleve（藥名）。

單字

rub	[rʌb]	揉
headache	[ˈhɛdˌek]	頭痛
often	[ˈɔfən]	時常
usually	[ˈjuʒʊəlɪ]	adv. 通常
relax	[rɪˈlæks]	放輕鬆
medicine	[ˈmɛdəsn̩]	藥

胃痛

MP3-43

Conversation 1:

A: My stomach doesn't feel so good.

（我的胃不太舒服。）

B: Did you eat something weird?

（你有沒有吃什麼比較特別的東西？）

A: I ate some shrimp by accident.

（我不小心吃了蝦子。）

I thought it was chicken.

（我以為那是雞。）

B: Ooh, I've never heard of that.

（噢，這我倒沒聽過。）

You don't like shrimp?

（你不喜歡蝦？）

A: No, I can't stand it.

（不是，我不可以吃。）

What would you do?

（你說我該怎麼辦？）

B: I guess I'd take some Pepto-Bismol and just lay down.

（我想我會吃 Pepto-Bismol，然後躺下來。）

Conversation 2:

A: You don't look too good.

（你看起來臉色不太好。）

B: I don't feel well.

（我覺得不舒服。）

My stomach hurts.

（我的胃很痛。）

A: Why is that?

（為什麼？）

B: I have no idea.

（我不知道。）

I just took some medicine.

（我剛吃了一些藥。）

A: You might want to take a break for a while.

（你可能要休息一會兒。）

B: Yah, I think you're right.

（是，我想你說的對。）

A: That Mexican food didn't agree with me.

My stomach's killing me.

B: Me too.

I don't think I'll go back to that place.

A: 那墨西哥食物使我胃不舒服。

我的胃痛的很。

B: 我也是。

我想我不會再回去那裡吃。

A: Do you have any medicine for an upset stomach?

B: Yah, I've got some Tums.

A: 你有沒有什麼吃胃痛的藥？

B: 有，我有一些 Tums.

A: Do you think Pepto-Bismol really works?

B: Absolutely.

A: 你認為 Pepto-Bismol 真的有效嗎？

B: 當然了。

A: What do you do when your stomach hurts?

B: I try to take some medicine and lay down.

A: 你胃痛時怎麼辦？

B: 我吃點藥，然後躺下。

stomach	[ˈstʌmək]	胃
weird	[wɪrd]	奇怪的
shrimp	[ʃrɪmp]	蝦
accident	[ˈæksədənt]	n. 意外事件
stand	[stænd]	v. 忍受
lay	[le]	躺著
hurt	[hɝt]	痛；傷害
agree	[əˈgri]	v. 同意；一致
upset	[ˈʌpˈsɛt]	不高興
absolutely	[ˈæbsəˌlutlɪ]	當然

43

感冒

MP3-44

Conversation 1:

A: You sound stuffed up.

（你聽起來有點鼻塞。）

B: I've got a cold.

（我感冒了。）

A: I think something's going around.

（我認為有什麼疾病在流行著。）

B: I wish I didn't catch it.

（我希望我沒傳染到。）

I feel terrible.

（我覺得很不舒服。）

A: Have you taken anything?

（你有沒有吃什麼藥？）

B: No, not yet.

（還沒。）

A: What's wrong with you?

（你怎麼啦？）

B: I've got a cold.

（我感冒了。）

A: You sound stopped up.

（你聽起來有點鼻塞。）

B: Yah, and my throat is sore.

（是，而且我的喉嚨痛。）

A: I feel sorry for you.

（我替你難過。）

B: Thanks.

（謝謝。）

More Practices:

A: You don't look so good.

B: I've got a cold.

A: 你看起來不太好。

B: 我感冒了。

A: What's wrong with you?

B: I think I caught a cold.

A: 你怎麼啦？

B: 我想我感冒了。

A: You sound pretty bad.

B: My throat is sore and I'm losing my voice.

> **A:** 你聽起來情況很糟。
> **B:** 我的喉嚨痛，快沒聲音了。

A: That's a pretty bad cough.

B: I know, it's killing me.

> **A:** 你的感冒很嚴重。
> **B:** 我知道，我非常不舒服。

單字

cold	[kold]	n. 感冒
catch	[kætʃ]	染上（疾病）
terrible	[ˈtɛrəbl̩]	（口語）糟透的；可怕的
throat	[θrot]	喉嚨
sore	[sor]	酸痛
voice	[vɔɪs]	n. 聲音
cough	[kɔf]	咳嗽

44

嘔吐

Conversation 1:

A: Are you okay?

（你還好嗎？）

B: No, I've been throwing up all night.

（不好，我整晚都在吐。）

A: Oh man, I'm sorry.

（噢，我替你難過。）

Do you want some soup or something?

（你要喝點湯或是什麼東西嗎？）

B: I just had some 7UP.

（我剛喝了七喜汽水。）

A: Let me know if you need anything.

（你如果需要什麼東西，讓我知道。）

B: Thanks.

（謝謝。）

Conversation 2:

A: You must have eaten something terrible.

（你一定吃了什麼不好的東西。）

B: I don't know what it is, but I can't keep anything down lately.

（我不知道那是什麼，但是我最近吃什麼東西都留不住。）

A: Have you been to the doctor?

（你有沒有去看醫生？）

B: Yah, he gave me some medicine.

（有，他給了我一些藥。）

More Practices:

A: Is she vomiting?

B: Yes, I think she ate something bad.

A: 她在吐嗎？

B: 是的，我想她吃了什麼不好的東西。

A: I heard Amy was sick.

B: She has the flu.

She's been throwing up all night.

A: 我聽説艾米病了。

B: 她患了重感冒。

她整晚都在吐。

A: You don't look good at all.

B: Tell me about it.

I've been throwing up all day.

A: 你看起來不太好。

B: 就是說嘛。

我一整天都在吐。

A: Can you make me something to eat?

I need something that won't upset my stomach.

B: Okay, I'll make you some chicken noodle soup.

A: 你可以煮點東西給我吃嗎？

我需要不會令我胃不舒服的。

B: 好，我可以煮點雞麵條湯。

單字

soup	[sup]	湯
terrible	[ˈtɛrəbl]	（口語）糟透的；可怕的
lately	[ˈletlɪ]	近來；最近的
vomit	[ˈvɑmɪt]	嘔吐
flu	[flu]	流行性感冒

Chapter 12

租賃英語

Unit

45

聯絡

MP3-46

Conversation 1:

A: Do you have any apartments available right now?

（你們現在有公寓可以出租嗎？）

B: Yes, we have several.

（有，我們有幾間有空。）

A: Could you send me a brochure on your facilities?

（你們可以寄有關你們的設施的小冊子給我嗎？）

B: No problem.

（沒問題。）

What is your current address?

（你的地址？）

A: 315 North Main.

（北緬因街 315 號。）

B: Okay, I'll send you the information.

（好的，我會把資料寄給你。）

A: Thank you for calling ABC Apartments.

（謝謝你打電話來 ABC 公寓。）

B: Hi, I'm trying to find a three-bedroom apartment.

（嗨，我在找三房的公寓。）

Do you have any available?

（你們有沒有可以出租的？）

A: No, I'm sorry.

（沒有，對不起。）

We don't at this time.

（目前沒有。）

We do have several two-bedroom apartments available.

（我們現在有幾間兩房的公寓。）

B: All right, thanks a lot.

（好的，謝謝。）

More Practices:

A: What do you have available right now?

B: We are full.

A: 你們現在有什麼公寓可以出租？

B: 我們都滿了。

A: Do you have any apartments available?

B: Yes, we have several to choose from.

> **A:** 你們有公寓可以出租嗎？
>
> **B:** 有，我們有幾間可以讓你選。

A: Could you send me a brochure in the mail?

B: No, we don't have any brochures, but we'd be happy to give you a tour.

> **A:** 你們可以寄小冊子給我嗎？
> **B:** 我們沒有小冊子，我們很樂意你來參觀。

A: Can I come by and pick up a brochure?

B: Sure, that would be great.

> **A:** 我可以過來拿本小冊子嗎？
> **B:** 沒問題，那很好。

單字

apartment	[əˈpɑrtmənt]	n. 公寓
available	[əˈveləbl̩]	可用的；現成可使用的
several	[ˈsɛvrəl]	幾個
brochure	[broˈʃʊr]	小冊子；說明書
facility	[fəˈsɪlətɪ]	設施
current	[ˈkɝənt]	目前的
information	[ˌɪnfɚˈmeʃən]	資料；資訊；訊息
choose	[tʃuz]	v. 選擇
mail	[mel]	郵寄
tour	[tʊr]	參觀

詢問租賃狀況

Conversation 1:

A: How much is a two-bedroom apartment?

（兩房的公寓多少錢？）

B: $450 a month.

（一個月四百五十塊美金。）

A: And a three-bedroom apartment?

（三房呢？）

B: $575.

（美金 575 元。）

A: Thanks a lot.

（多謝。）

Conversation 2:

A: How large are your two-bedroom apartments?

（你們的兩房公寓有多大？）

B: They are about 1000 square feet.

（大約一千呎。）

We have some that have an extra bathroom and that bumps it up a little.

（我們有幾間有多一間浴室，那就更大一點。）

A: Do the apartments have a fireplace?

（你們的公寓有壁爐嗎？）

B: Only on the second floor.

（只有二樓有。）

A: Are they extra?

（是另外算錢嗎？）

B: Yes, it adds about $20 a month.

（是的，每個月多二十元。）

More Practices:

A: Do the apartments have a washer and dryer?

B: Yes, they do.

    A: 你們的公寓有洗衣機和烘乾機嗎？

    B: 有。

A: How close are restaurants to the apartments?

B: We have several restaurants nearby.

    A: 餐廳離你們的公寓有多遠？
    B: 有幾家餐廳在這附近。

A: Does the apartment complex have a pool?

B: Yes, we actually have two.

> **A:** 你們社區有游泳池嗎？
> **B:** 有，我們有兩個游泳池。

A: How much is it to get a covered parking space?

B: That's part of your rent.

> **A:** 要個有頂棚的停車位要多少錢？
> **B:** 有頂棚的停車位包括在你們的租金之內。

單字

month	[mʌnθ]	月
large	[lɑrdʒ]	大的
square	[skwɛr]	（數學）平方
feet	[fit]	呎
bump	[bʌmp]	提高
fireplace	['faɪrples]	n. 火爐
add	[æd]	加
washer	['wɑʃɚ]	n. 洗衣機
dryer	['draɪɚ]	烘乾機
close	[klos]	a. 接近
restaurant	['rɛstərənt]	n. 餐館；飯店
nearby	['nɪr'baɪ]	附近
complex	['kɑmplɛks]	（同性質建築）一區
pool	[pul]	n. 游泳池
space	[spes]	空間；空地
rent	[rɛnt]	出租；租金

47 請朋友幫忙

Conversation 1:

A: Do you know of any good apartments?

（你知不知道有什麼好的公寓？）

B: Not really, why?

（不知道，為什麼要問？）

A: We're looking to move pretty soon.

（我們很快就要搬家。）

B: Oh.

（噢。）

What are you looking for?

（你們在找什麼樣的公寓？）

A: We want a two-bedroom place.

（我們要一間兩房的。）

B: All right.

（好的。）

I'll keep my eyes open.

（我會幫你們留意。）

A: Could you do me a favor?

（你能不能幫我一個忙？）

B: Sure, what do you need?

（可以，你需要什麼？）

A: We're looking for a new place.

（我們在找一個新的地方住。）

Could you keep your eyes open for a two-bedroom apartment?

（你能不能幫忙留意兩房的公寓。）

B: No problem.

（沒問題。）

When do you want to move?

（你什麼時候要搬？）

A: Any time.

（隨時都可以搬。）

B: Okay.

（好的。）

More Practices:

A: Keep watch for a good apartment to rent.

B: Sure thing.

A: 留意看看有什麼好的公寓要出租？

B: 沒問題。

A: What type of place are you looking for?

B: Something cheap.

Around $300.

A: 你在找什麼樣的地方？

B: 便宜一點的。

大約美金三百元左右。

A: Let me know if you see any nice places to rent.

B: Okay.

A: 如果你看到什麼好的地方出租，跟我說一聲。

B: 好的。

A: Can you be on the lookout for a nice apartment for us?

B: Sure.

I'll tell you if I see anything.

A: 你可不可以替我們留意有什麼好的公寓出租？

B: 好的。

如果看到什麼好的，我會告訴你。

單字

favor	['fevɚ]	（美語）幫忙
rent	[rɛnt]	出租；租金
cheap	[tʃip]	a. 便宜的
nice	[naɪs]	很好
lookout	['lʊkaʊt]	留意觀察

談判租賃條件

Conversation 1:

A: How much are you asking for the apartment?

（你的公寓出租要多少錢？）

B: $550 a month.

（一個月美金五百五十元。）

A: Hmm, that sounds a little high.

（聽起來價錢有點高。）

All of the other places in the area are going for around $475.

（所有這一區其他的公寓都要求在美金四百七十五元左右。）

B: Well, I can work with you a little bit, but not that much.

（我的價錢還稍微可以商量，但是沒辦法降那麼多。）

You can see that these apartments are the nicest in the area.

（你可以看得出來，我這裡的公寓是這附近最好的。）

A: I could probably take it if you could get it down to $520 a month.

（如果你能降到一個月美金五百二十元，我就租了。）

B: How does $525 sound?

（美金一個月美金五百二十五元，怎麼樣？）

Conversation 2:

A: I'm really interested in the place but I'm concerned that the rent is a little too high.

（我對這地方很有興趣，但是我考慮租金好像貴了一點。）

B: Well, I'm confident that this place is worth every penny I'm asking.

（我很有信心，這地方值得我所要的每一分價錢。）

Some places are higher.

（有些地方還貴一點呢。）

A: I know, but I really need to be paying about $50 less than what you're asking.

（我知道，但是我只能付你所要求的再少美金五十元。）

B: Well, I'd love to rent you the apartment, but I'm not able to negotiate the price with you.

（我很想把公寓租給你，但是我沒辦法跟你商量價錢。）

You can have the apartment, but the price is fixed.

（你可以租這個公寓，但是價錢是固定的。）

A: Okay, I'll have to think about it and get back with you.

（好，我考慮看看，再跟你説。）

B: No problem.

（沒問題。）

I'll look for your call.

（我等你的電話。）

More Practices:

A: Do you offer discounts for students?

B: Yes, we offer a 5% discount.

    A: 對學生你們有沒有打折優待？

    B: 有，我們給學生打九五折。

A: I really like the apartment, but I think $400 sounds more reasonable than $450.

B: Well, I guess I could take that.

    A: 我很喜歡這個公寓，但是我認為美金四百元比四百五十元更合理。

    B: 我想這個價錢我可以接受。

A: How much flexibility do you have in the rent

price?

B: None at all.

> **A:** 你們的租金還有多少商量的餘地？
> **B:** 沒有商量的餘地。

A: Do you think you could save me about $10 a month on the rent payment?

B: No, the price is fixed.

> **A:** 你想你可以每個月替我省個十塊錢美金嗎？
> **B:** 不行，價錢是固定的。

單字

area	[ˈɛrɪə]	地區
sound	[saʊnd]	v. 聽起來
concerned	[kənˈsɝnd]	關切的；擔心的
confident	[ˈkɑnfədənt]	a. 自信的；確信
penny	[ˈpɛnɪ]	一分錢
less	[lɛs]	較少的
negotiate	[nɪˈgoʃɪ͵et]	談判
fixed	[fɪkst]	固定的
price	[praɪs]	價格
discount	[dɪsˈkaʊnt]	v. 打折
offer	[ˈɔfɚ]	v. 提供
reasonable	[ˈriznəbl]	合理的
flexibility	[flɛksəˈbɪlətɪ]	變通性
save	[sev]	節省

Chapter 13

新科技英語

個人電腦

MP3-50

Conversation 1:

A: I heard you got a new computer.

（我聽説你買了一部新電腦。）

B: It's true.

（是啊。）

I got it yesterday.

（我昨天買的。）

A: What is it?

（你買了什麼型號的電腦？）

B: It's an HP 6370Z.

（是 HP6370Z。）

Pretty quick.

（是很快的電腦。）

More Practices:

A: How do you like your computer?

B: I hate it.

The hard drive is so small I can barely save a letter.

A: 你喜歡你的電腦嗎？

B: 不喜歡。

硬碟太小了，我幾乎連存封信都不行。

A: Did you buy a printer with your computer?

B: No, I already had one.

A: 你買電腦時，有沒有買印表機？

B: 沒有，我已經有一個印表機了。

A: How much was your whole system?

B: With the computer, monitor, and printer it was almost two grand.

A: 你買的整套電腦系統共多少錢？

B: 包括電腦主機，監控器和印表機，差不多兩千美元。

單字

computer	[kəm'pjutɚ]	n. 電腦
quick	[kwɪk]	a. 快的；迅速的
barely	['bɛrlɪ]	adv. 幾乎不能
save	[sev]	儲存
printer	[prɪntɚ]	印表機
whole	[hol]	全部的
system	['sɪstəm]	系統
grand	[grænd]	一千美元

50

網際網路

Conversation 1:

A: What service do you have for the Internet?
（你的網際網路用哪一家的？）

B: GTE.
（GTE。）

A: How much is it?
（一個月多少錢？）

B: It's about $20 a month.
（一個月大約美金二十元。）

A: Do you like it?
（你喜歡嗎？）

B: It's okay, but it seems a little expensive.
（還好，但是有點太貴。）

Conversation 2:

A: What do you use the Internet for?
（你用網際網路來做什麼？）

B: Mostly for research or to check sports scores.

（大部分用來查球賽分數。）

A: See, I don't do any of that stuff.

（我不做那些事。）

All I do is order books online.

（我都是用來做線上買書。）

B: Hmm.

（嗯。）

A: And I don't know if it's really worth paying every month just to order stuff.

（我不知道每個月付那些錢用來買書是否值得。）

B: I don't know.

（我不知道。）

I guess that's up to you.

（我想要你自己來決定。）

More Practices:

A: Who's your service provider?

B: I use America Online.

A: 你用哪一家來進網際網路？

B: 我用『美國線上』。

A: Do you use the Internet much?

B: All the time.

I use it every day.

A: 你常上網際網路嗎？

B: 常常上。

我每天都用。

A: Are you going to get an Internet connection?

B: No, I don't use it enough.

A: 你要訂 Internet 連線嗎？

B: 不，我不常用。

單字

service	['sɝvɪs]	服務
seem	[sim]	似乎
expensive	[ɪk'spɛnsɪv]	昂貴的
sports	[spɔrts]	運動的
score	[skor]	分數
research	[rɪ'sɝtʃ]	研究
mostly	['mostlɪ]	多半
stuff	[stʌf]	n. 事情
order	['ɔrdɚ]	v. 訂購
worth	[wɝθ]	價值
provider	[prə'vaɪdɚ]	供應者
connection	[kə'nɛkʃən]	連接
enough	[ɪ'nʌf]	足夠的

電子郵件

Conversation 1:

A: I got this funny e-mail the other day.

（前幾天我收到一封很好玩的電子郵件。）

I ought to send it to you.

（我應該寄給你。）

B: Do you have my address?

（你有我的電子郵件地址嗎？）

A: No, I don't think I do.

（沒有。）

B: Okay, it's joek@yahoo.com.

（我的網址是 joek@yahoo.com。）

A: All right.

（好的。）

Conversation 2:

A: How often do you check your e-mail?

（你多常察看你的電子郵件？）

B: Not very often.

（不常。）

Only two or three times a week.

（一個星期兩三次。）

A: Man, I check mine all the time.

（我一天到晚在查。）

B: Yah, but you sit in front of a computer all day long.

（是啊，但是你一整天都坐在電腦前面。）

I have to go to the other room to check my e-mail.

（我必須到另外一間房間才能查電子郵件。）

Sometimes I just don't think about it.

（有時，我根本沒想到要去查。）

A: That makes sense.

（有道理。）

More Practices:

A: Do you have e-mail?

B: Yah, my address is rob@hotmail.com.

A: 你有電子郵件嗎？

B: 有，我的網址是 rob@hotmail.com。

A: What's your e-mail address?

B: tam@yahoo.com.

> **A:** 你的電子郵件網址是什麼？
>
> **B:** tam@yahoo.com。

A: Do you have an e-mail address?

B: No, we're switching Internet services right now.

> **A:** 你有電子郵件網址嗎？
>
> **B:** 沒有，我現在正在換另一家 Internet 公司。

A: Do you have my address?

B: Yah, I put it in my address book.

> **A:** 你有我的電子郵件網址嗎？
>
> **B:** 有，我把它放在我的網址簿上。

單字

funny	['fʌnɪ]	奇怪的；滑稽
address	[ə'drɛs]	n. 網址
check	[tʃɛk]	n. 查一查
front	[frʌnt]	前面
sometimes	['sʌm'taɪmz]	有時
switch	[swɪtʃ]	改變

Chapter 14

選舉英語

52

談候選人

Conversation 1:

A: Have you paid much attention to the election?

（你有在注意選舉嗎？）

B: I've been following it pretty well.

（我一直在留意一切。）

A: What do you think about Johnson?

（你認為強生怎麼樣？）

B: I agree with him on a lot of things, but I cannot see public funding of abortion.

（他的許多論點我都很同意，但是他對墮胎的觀點得不到大眾的支持。）

A: Yah, that's where he's going to lose a lot of votes.

（是，那是他會失去許多選票的一點。）

B: If he sticks with that, there's no way I will vote for him.

（如果他堅持那一點，我沒辦法投給他。）

A: What do you think about the election?

（這次選舉你認為怎麼樣？）

B: I'm pretty upset that the candidates are not talking about the issues.

（我很生氣，候選人都不談問題。）

A: Me too.

（我也是。）

I wish they would say what they are for instead of slamming the other guy so much.

（我希望他們能夠說他們的政見，而不只是在攻擊對方。）

B: I guess that's just the nature of politics.

（我想那就是政治吧。）

A: I don't know.

（我不知道。）

I don't think it has to be that way.

（我不認為政治一定要那樣。）

More Practices:

A: Do you think Smith will win the election?

B: I don't think he's got a chance in the world.

A: 你認為史密斯會贏嗎？

B: 我不認為他有任何機會。

A: This election's really heating up, huh?

B: I'll say.

I'm really interested to hear the debate this weekend.

> **A:** 選戰真的越來越激烈。
>
> **B:** 就是嘛！
>
> 我很有興趣聽這個週末的辯論。

A: What do you think of Jordan's policies?

B: I think she's on the right track.

> **A:** 你認為喬登的政見怎麼樣？
>
> **B:** 我認為她的方向很對。

A: Do you think Williams can beat Young?

B: I don't know, they both have some good ideas.

> **A:** 你認為威廉能夠擊敗楊格嗎？
>
> **B:** 我不知道，他們兩個都有很好的主意。

單字

attention	[ə'tɛnʃən]	n. 注意；注意力
election	[ɪ'lɛkʃən]	選舉
follow	['fɑlo]	注意（事件的）發展

public	['pʌblɪk]	公用的；公共的
funding	['fʌndɪŋ]	資助
abortion	[ə'bɔrʃən]	墮胎
vote	[vot]	投票
stick	[stɪk]	v. 執著於
candidate	['kændə,det]	候選人
issue	['ɪʃju]	問題
slam	[slæm]	猛烈評擊
nature	['netʃɚ]	n. 天性
politics	['pɑlə,tɪks]	政治
win	[wɪn]	贏
debate	[dɪ'bet]	辯論
policy	['pɑləsɪ]	政策
track	[træk]	軌道

你要投票給誰

MP3-54

Conversation 1:

A: Are you following the election?

（你有在注意選情嗎？）

B: You bet.

（當然囉。）

A: Whom are you going to vote for?

（你要投票給誰？）

B: Bush.

（布希。）

I think he can really help us out.

（我認為他能幫助我們。）

What about you?

（你呢？）

A: I'm not decided yet.

（我還沒有決定。）

I need to do a little more digging.

（我還需要研究研究。）

B: That's good that you're really exploring the issues.

（你能真正去探討問題，是很好的。）

Conversation 2:

A: So who's going to get your vote this year?

（你今年的票要投給誰？）

B: I'm going to vote for Smith.

（我要投給史密斯。）

A: Are you serious?

（真的嗎？）

B: Yes.

（是啊。）

I know she won't win, but I honestly think she's the best person for the job.

（我知道她不會贏，但是，我真心相信她可以做得很好。）

A: Better than White?

（比懷特還好？）

B: No contest.

（他根本比不上。）

White's all talk.

（懷特只會說，根本不會做事。）

A: Whom are you going to vote for?

B: I haven't made up my mind yet.

> **A:** 你將投票給誰？
>
> **B:** 我還沒決定。

A: Do you know whom you're going to vote?

B: I'm voting for Parks.

> **A:** 你知道你要投票給誰嗎？
> **B:** 我要投給派克斯。

A: Whom do you think you'll vote for?

B: Probably Kennedy unless he does something stupid in the next week or two.

> **A:** 你想你會投票給誰？
> **B:** 可能會投給甘迺迪，除非接下來的一、兩個星期裡他出了什麼差錯。

單字

vote	[vot]	投票
decide	[dɪˈsaɪd]	v. 決定
digging	[ˈdɪgɪŋ]	挖掘
explore	[ɪkˈsplor]	考察；探索
honestly	[ˈɑnəstlɪ]	老實的
contest	[ˈkɑntɛst]	n. 競爭
mind	[maɪnd]	頭腦
stupid	[ˈstjupɪd]	愚；蠢
unless	[ənˈlɛs]	除非

54

投票結果

Conversation 1:

A: How many people voted this year?

（今年有多少人投票？）

B: We had a really good turnout.

（今年的投票率不錯。）

About 70% voted.

（大約有百分之七十的人投票。）

A: That's better than in the past.

（那比往年好。）

B: I know.

（我知道。）

I'm pretty satisfied.

（我很滿意。）

Conversation 2:

A: Did you hear about the turnout for the election?

（你有沒有聽說投票率是多少？）

B: No.

（沒有。）

A: They said that 70,000 people voted.

（他們説有七萬人投票。）

That's almost 20%.

（那大約是百分之二十。）

B: That's pitiful.

（真是糟。）

Can you believe how hard people fight for the right to vote and then they don't even vote?

（你知道以前的人，費盡多少心力才得到投票權，現在他們卻不去投票。）

A: It doesn't make much sense to me.

（我也搞不懂。）

B: I don't think I'll ever understand it.

（我不認為我會瞭解是怎麼一回事。）

More Practices:

A: What was the turnout this year?

B: About 40%.

A: 今年的投票率是多少？

B: 大約百分之四十。

A: I wonder how many people will vote this year.

B: Who knows?

Not enough though.

A: 不知道今年有多少人會投票。

B: 誰知道？

總之不會太多人。

A: What percentage of the population votes?

B: About 35% I'd say.

A: 投票率是多少？

B: 我猜大約百分之三十五。

A: Was the voter turnout good this year?

B: It was pretty good, but it could always be a lot better.

A: 今年的投票率好不好？

B: 很不錯，但是還是有加強的地方。

單字

turnout	[ˈtɜnˌoʊt]	投票人
past	[pæst]	n. 過去
satisfied	[ˈsaɪtɪsfaɪd]	滿意的
pitiful	[ˈpɪtəfəl]	可憐的
fight	[faɪt]	奮鬥
right	[raɪt]	n. 權利
sense	[sɛns]	道理
population	[ˌpɑpjəˈleʃən]	n. 人口
percentage	[pɚˈsɛntɪdʒ]	百分比；百分率

政黨

MP3-56

Conversation 1:

A: Are you a Republican or a Democrat?

（你是民主黨還是共和黨？）

B: Why do you ask?

（你為什麼要問？）

A: Just curious.

（只是好奇。）

B: Well, I don't consider myself to be either one.

（我兩黨都不是。）

I think you should vote on the person, not the party.

（我認為你應該選人不選黨。）

A: That's true, but not many people do that.

（那也對，但不是很多人這麼做。）

B: I know.

（我知道。）

Most people don't even know what the issues are.

（大多數人甚至於不知道問題是什麼。）

Conversation 2:

A: Are you a member of a party?

（你有入黨嗎？）

B: I'm a card carrying Republican.

（我是有黨證的共和黨人。）

A: Do you always vote Republican?

（你總是投給共和黨的候選人嗎？）

B: Let me put it this way.

（我來告訴你吧。）

I always vote for who I think will do the best job, and I've never voted for a Democrat.

（我總是投給我認為最好的人，結果是我還沒有一次投給民主黨的候選人。）

A: That's hard to believe.

（真是難以相信。）

More Practices:

A: Are you a Republican or a Democrat?

B: A Democrat.

A: 你是共和黨還是民主黨？

B: 民主黨。

A: Do you belong to a party?

B: No, but I usually vote Libertarian.

> **A:** 你有入黨嗎？
>
> **B:** 沒有，但是我通常投給自由黨。

A: How do you usually vote?

B: I'd say it's 50-50 Republican and Democrat.

> **A:** 你通常都怎麼投票？
> **B:** 我投給民主黨和共和黨各半。

單字

curious	[ˈkjʊrɪəs]	a. 好奇的
consider	[kənˈsɪdɚ]	v. 認為
myself	[maɪˈsɛlf]	我自己
either	[ˈiðɚ]	a.〔兩者中之〕任一
party	[ˈpɑrtɪ]	政黨
member	[ˈmɛmbɚ]	會員
carry	[ˈkærɪ]	攜帶
usually	[ˈjuʒʊəlɪ]	adv. 通常

Chapter 15

辦公室英語

56

要求幫忙

Conversation 1:

A: Are you busy right now?

（你現在忙嗎？）

B: I'm always busy.

（我總是很忙。）

Do you need something?

（你需要什麼嗎？）

A: Yes, I'm having trouble understanding these numbers.

（是的，這些數字我不瞭解。）

B: I guess nobody told you.

（我猜沒有人告訴你吧。）

All the numbers are goofed up.

（所有的數目都是亂七八糟的。）

A: No wonder.

（難怪。）

A: Could you give me a hand here?

（你可以幫我一個忙嗎？）

B: Sure, what do you need?

（可以，你需要什麼？）

A: I can't get the computer to download this file.

（我沒辦法從電腦下載一個檔案。）

B: I see what's wrong.

（我知道哪裡出問題了。）

The cable is cut.

（纜線斷了。）

I'll get you a new one.

（我替你拿一條新的。）

More Practices:

A: Can you help me run some numbers?

B: Yah, give me a minute.

A: 你可以幫我算一些數目嗎？

B: 好的，稍等一下。

A: I need to run an errand.

Can you cover for me for a bit?

B: No problem.

A: 我需要去辦一些雜務。

你可以幫我照看一下嗎？

B: 沒問題。

A: Do you know where the new project assignments are?

B: Yah, John's bringing them around.

    A: 你知道新派下來的企畫在哪裡嗎？

    B: 知道，約翰把它們帶在身上。

A: I need some help with my computer.

B: Okay, I'll send tech support out.

    A: 我需要有人來幫我解決電腦的問題。

    B: 好的，我會派技術人員過去。

單字

busy	[ˈbɪzɪ]	忙的
trouble	[ˈtrʌbl̩]	麻煩；困難
number	[ˈnʌmbɚ]	數字
download	[ˈdaʊnˈlod]	下載
file	[faɪl]	檔案
cable	[ˈkebl̩]	電纜
cut	[kʌt]	砍斷
errand	[ˈɛrənd]	雜務事
cover	[ˈkʌvɚ]	（口語）代班
project	[ˈprɑdʒɛkt]	專案；企畫
assignment	[əˈsaɪnmənt]	n. 指定的工作
tech	[tɛk]	科技
support	[səˈpɔrt]	支持

57

升遷

MP3-58

Conversation 1:

A: I heard you got a promotion.

（我聽說你得到升遷。）

B: You heard right.

（沒錯。）

A: Congratulations.

（恭喜。）

Are you excited?

（你覺得興奮嗎？）

B: Kind of.

（有一點。）

It's really just a change in title.

（只是頭銜上的改變而已。）

I've been doing all the work for a while now.

（那些工作我已經做了好一段時間了。）

A: I bet the extra cash can't hurt.

（我猜多一點錢也無妨。）

B: That's for sure.

（那當然囉。）

Conversation 2:

A: When are you up for a promotion?

（你什麼時候會升遷？）

B: They're supposed to do my yearly review tomorrow.

（他們明天要做年度審核。）

A: Do you think you'll get it?

（你想你會得到升遷嗎？）

B: I better.

（我最好能拿到。）

I've been working a lot of extra hours around here.

（我一直加很多班。）

More Practices:

A: Congratulations on the promotion.

B: Thanks, I'm really happy.

> **A:** 恭喜你得到升遷。
>
> **B:** 謝謝，我真的很高興。

A: I heard you didn't get the promotion.

B: Yah, I'm pretty ticked off.

> **A:** 我聽説你沒得到升遷。
>
> **B:** 是的，我很生氣。

A: Can you believe John got a promotion?

B: Not at all.

He's the laziest guy around here.

> **A:** 你會相信約翰竟然得到升遷嗎？
>
> **B:** 我真的不相信。
>
> 他是這裡最懶惰的人。

A: I heard you got the promotion.

Way to go.

B: Thanks.

> **A:** 我聽説你得到升遷了。
>
> 很不錯。
>
> **B:** 謝謝。

單字

promotion	[prə'moʃən]	升遷
congratulations	[kən͵grætʃə'leʃənz]	恭喜
title	['taɪtl̩]	n. 頭銜
cash	[kæʃ]	n. 現金
review	[rɪ'vju]	審核

Conversation 1:

A: Did you hear about the raise?
（你有沒有聽説加薪的事？）

B: No, what's the deal?
（沒有，是怎麼回事？）

A: Everyone should get a 10% raise this year.
（今年每個人加薪百分之十。）

B: That's great.
（好棒。）

Conversation 2:

A: Guess what!
（你猜是什麼事？）

B: What?
（什麼事？）

A: I got a raise at work today.
（今天我得到加薪。）

B: That's great.

（那很棒。）

How much?

（加多少？）

A: You're not going to believe this, $10,000.

（你不會相信的，年薪加美金一萬元。）

B: Wow!

（哇。）

More Practices:

A: How much was your raise?

B: Just 3%.

A: 你加薪加了多少？

B: 加百分之三。

A: Why aren't they giving raises this year?

B: I have no idea.

They always have in the past.

A: 今年為什麼沒有加薪？

B: 我不知道。

往年都有加薪的。

A: Did you get a raise?

B: Yes, but it's not that much.

> **A:** 你有沒有得到加薪？
>
> **B:** 有，但是不多。

A: I heard you got a big raise.

B: It's true.

Not only did I get a raise, but you're looking at the new Assistant Director.

> **A:** 我聽說你加薪加很多。
>
> **B:** 是真的。
>
> 我不僅得到加薪，你眼前這個人還是個新的副主管。

單字

raise	[rez]	v. 加薪
should	[ʃʊd]	應該

Chapter 16

交通工具

搭飛機

Conversation 1:

A: When are you leaving for Houston?

（你什麼時候去休士頓？）

B: Tomorrow at 6:30.

（明天六點半。）

The flight should only take about an hour.

（飛行只要半小時。）

A: I thought you were driving.

（我原本以為你要開車。）

B: No, I got a ticket for about $100 and decided to fly.

（沒有，機票只要美金一百元，所以我決定搭飛機。）

A: That will be nice.

（那很好。）

B: Yah, I think so.

（是啊，我是這麼想。）

A: I need to book a flight for Hong Kong on the 6th.

（我要訂一張六號到香港的機票。）

B: Round trip or one way?

（來回票或是單程票？）

A: Round trip.

（來回票。）

I'd like to go first class.

（我要頭等艙。）

B: All right.

（好的。）

We have three first class flights to Hong Kong on the 6th: one at 10, one at 3 and one at 6:30.

（到香港的班機有三班有頭等艙的空位，一班是十點，一班在三點，還有一班在六點半。）

A: How about the 6:30 flight?

（我想要六點半的。）

B: Okay.

（好的。）

More Practices:

A: Do you fly round trip to New York?

B: Certainly.

A: 你買來回機票去紐約嗎？

B: 是的。

A: Where does your flight leave from?

B: Gate 23.

A: 你的班機從哪裡起飛？

B: 23 號登機門。

A: Would you prefer an aisle seat or a window seat?

B: Window, please.

A: 你想要靠走道還是靠窗的座位？

B: 靠窗。

A: How long is the flight to San Francisco?

B: About three hours.

A: 到舊金山要飛多久？

B: 大約三小時。

單字

leave	[liv]	離開
flight	[flaɪt]	班機
fly	[flaɪ]	搭機旅行
round trip		來回
certainly	[ˈsɝtn̩lɪ]	當然；當然可以
aisle	[aɪl]	走道
seat	[sit]	座位

搭公車

Conversation 1:

A: Do you have any seats on the bus to New York City for tonight?

（今晚到紐約的公車還有座位嗎？）

B: Yes, we still have several seats.

（有，還有好幾個座位。）

A: Good, how much is that ticket?

（很好，票價多少？）

B: It's $42 one way or $78 round trip.

（單程四十二元，來回票七十八元。）

A: I just need a one way ticket.

（我只需要一張單程票。）

B: All right, that'll be $42 then.

（好的，那是四十二元。）

Conversation 2:

A: Have you ever taken a bus trip before?

（你有沒有坐公車旅行過？）

B: Yes, but I didn't like it.

（有，但是我不喜歡。）

A: Why not?

（為什麼不喜歡？）

B: Oh, it just took so long and it wasn't all that comfortable.

（噢，坐太久了，而且一點也不舒服。）

A: That makes sense.

（那有道理。）

More Practices:

A: Do you have any seats available on the bus?

B: No.

A: 你們還有座位嗎？

B: 沒有了。

A: Does the bus have a restroom on it?

B: Yes sir, it does.

A: 公車上有洗手間嗎？

B: 有。

A: I need three tickets for tonight's bus to Boston.

B: Okay, it'll be $186.

> **A:** 我要三張今晚到波士頓的車票。
> **B:** 好的，總共是一百八十六元。

A: How much is a ticket to Taipei?

B: $125.

> **A:** 到台北的票價是多少？
>
> **B:** 一百二十五元。

單字

trip	[trɪp]	旅程；旅遊
comfortable	[ˈkʌmfɚtəbl̩]	a. 舒適的
restroom	[ˈrɛstrum]	洗手間

61

搭火車

MP3-62

Conversation 1:

A: How do you want to get around in Washington?
（你在華盛頓時要怎麼外出？）

By taxi?
（搭計程車嗎？）

B: No, I heard that the subway is the best way to go.
（不，我聽說搭地鐵是最好的方法。）

A: I wonder how much it costs.
（不知道要多少錢。）

B: Probably about 50 cents.
（大約五十分錢一趟路。）

I don't know though.
（我不太清楚。）

A: I bet it's more than that.
（我猜應該會更貴。）

B: It could be.
（可能吧。）

A: Have you ever been on a train?

（你有沒有搭過火車？）

B: Yes, I rode a train from Dallas all the way to Los Angeles.

（有，我從達拉斯一路坐到洛杉磯。）

A: I bet that took forever.

（我敢說，一定坐很久。）

B: It did.

（是啊。）

We left here around midnight and got there two days later.

（我們大約半夜時離開，兩天後才到達那裡。）

A: Did you have a sleeper car?

（你們坐的有睡艙嗎？）

B: No, we had to sleep in our chairs.

（沒有，我們在椅子上睡。）

More Practices:

A: Do you like riding on the subway?

B: Yeah, but I get worried sometimes since it's dangerous.

A: 你喜歡搭地鐵嗎？

B: 喜歡，但是我有時會擔心，因為怕危險。

A: Can you take a train from Boston straight to New York?

B: I'm not sure.

　A: 你可以從波士頓直接坐火車到紐約嗎？

　B: 我不太清楚。

A: Do you think a train is cheaper than flying?

B: Oh yeah.

　A: 你認為搭火車會比搭飛機便宜嗎？

　B: 是啊。

單字

taxi	['tæksɪ]	計程車
subway	['sʌb,we]	地下鐵
cost	[kɔst]	v. 花費
though	[ðo]	（口語）不過
train	[tren]	火車
forever	[fɚ'ɛvɚ]	永久的
dangerous	['dendʒərəs]	a. 危險的

62

搭計程車

Conversation 1:

A: Taxi!!

（計程車。）

B: Hello, where to?

（哈囉，要去哪裡？）

A: The Central Park.

（中央公園。）

B: I know the place.

（我知道那地方。）

Conversation 2:

A: Taxi!!

（計程車。）

B: Hi.

（嗨。）

A: How many people can ride back here?

（幾個人可以搭回來這裡？）

B: It's the same price for up to four people.

（四個人以下都是同樣的價錢。）

A: Good, that will help us out a lot.

（好，那可幫了我們大忙。）

More Practices:

A: Here you are.

It's $10.50.

B: Okay, here's $12.

Keep the change.

    A: 到了，車資十塊五毛。

    B: 好的，這是十二元，不用找了。

A: Taxi!!

Hi, I need to go downtown.

B: No problem.

    A: 計程車。嗨，我要到市中心去。

    B: 好的。

A: Can you take me to the train station?

B: You got it.

A: 你可不可以帶我到火車站去？
B: 可以。

A: Where to today?

B: The Central park.

A: 要去哪裡？

B: 中央公園。

taxi	['tækɪ]	計程車
ride	[raɪd]	搭載
downtown	['daʊn'taʊn]	市區；市中心
station	['steʃən]	車站

63

開車

Conversation 1:

A: Do you want a ride?

（你要搭我的車嗎？）

B: Sure.

（好的。）

Thanks.

（謝謝。）

A: No problem, I'm going right by your house anyway.

（沒問題，我反正會經過你家。）

B: I thought your office was on the other side of town.

（我以為你的辦公室在另一邊。）

A: It is, but I carpool with John.

（是的，但是我跟約翰共乘一部車上班。）

B: Oh, that's good.

（噢，那很好。）

A: Can you give me a ride?

（你能載我嗎？）

B: Where are you headed?

（你要去哪裡？）

A: To the grocery store.

（到雜貨店去。）

B: All right, I can do that.

（好的，可以。）

A: Thanks a lot.

（謝謝。）

More Practices:

A: John, the maintenance light came on in the car.

B: Yeah, it's time to get the oil changed.

A: 約翰，車子的維修燈亮了。

B: 是的，是該換機油的時候了。

A: How much gas do you have?

B: A quarter of a tank.

A: 你有多少汽油？

B: 四分之一滿。

A: How do you like your new car?

B: I love it.

It's really roomy.

A: 你喜歡你的新車嗎？

B: 喜歡。很寬敞。

A: How much was your car?

B: It's $330 a month.

A: 你的車子多少錢？

B: 一個月要付三百三十元。

單字

ride	[raɪd]	搭載
anyway	[ˈɛnɪˌwe]	反正
side	[saɪd]	一邊
town	[taʊn]	城市；城鎮
carpool	[karpul]	共乘一部車
maintenance	[ˈmentɪnəns]	維修
light	[laɪt]	燈
tank	[tæŋk]	油箱

Chapter 17

使用洗手間

Conversation 1:

A: Do you have a public restroom?

（你們有公用廁所嗎？）

B: Yes, it's near the back of the store.

（有，在店裡後面。）

A: Does it have handicapped access?

（有給殘障者進出的入口嗎？）

My mom is in a wheel chair.

（我的母親使用輪椅。）

B: Yes, it sure does.

（有。）

A: Great.

（很好。）

Thanks for your help.

（謝謝你。）

A: Where is your restroom?

（你們的洗手間在哪裡？）

B: We don't have a public restroom.

（我們沒有公用廁所。）

A: Do you know where one is?

（你知道哪裡有嗎？）

B: There's one near the Food Court.

（在飲食區附近有洗手間。）

A: Okay, thanks.

（好的，謝謝。）

More Practices:

A: Could you point me toward the restroom?

B: It's around the corner on the right.

A: 你能告訴我洗手間往哪裡走嗎？

B: 洗手間在轉角處在右邊。

A: Do you have a restroom?

B: Yes, but it's out of order.

A: 你們有洗手間嗎？

B: 有，但是，壞了。

A: Where is your restroom?

B: On the second floor next to customer service.

A: 你們的洗手間在哪裡？

B: 在二樓，在顧客服務處的旁邊。

單字

public	['pʌblɪk]	公用的；公共的
near	[nɪr]	靠近
back	[bæk]	後面
handicapped	['hædɪ,kæpt]	殘障的
access	['æksɛs]	進入
wheel	[whil]	輪子
wheel chair		輪椅
corner	['kɔrnɚ]	n. 角落；角
next to		在 ... 隔壁
customer	['kʌstəmɚ]	n. 顧客
service	['sɝvɪs]	服務

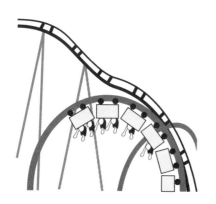

在別人家裡

Conversation 1:

A: Do you mind if I use your bathroom?

（我可以用你家的洗手間嗎？）

B: No, go ahead.

（可以，請便。）

A: Where is it?

（在哪裡？）

B: I'm sorry, I forgot this was your first time over here.

（對不起，我忘了你是第一次來。）

It's down the hall on your left.

（從走道下去，在你的左邊。）

A: Thanks

（謝謝。）

Conversation 2:

A: You sure are fidgeting a lot.

（你怎麼一副坐立難安的樣子。）

B: I know.

（我知道。）

I need to go to the bathroom.

（我需要去上廁所。）

A: Why didn't you say so?

（你為什麼不說？）

The bathroom is down the hall on the right.

（浴室從走道下去，在你的右邊。）

B: Okay, I just didn't want to be rude.

（好的，我剛剛只是不想太無禮。）

A: Rude, who are you kidding?

（無禮，開什麼玩笑？）

That's not rude.

（用個洗手間怎麼會無禮？）

More Practices:

A: Do you mind if I use the restroom?

B: No, go ahead.

    A: 我可以使用你家的洗手間嗎？

    B: 可以，請便。

A: Can you show me to the restroom?

B: Sure, it's this way.

> **A:** 請告訴我到洗手間怎麼走？
> **B:** 好的，走這裡。

A: Is it okay to use the restroom?

B: Sure, you can use mine.

> **A:** 我可以使用洗手間嗎？
> **B:** 可以，你可以用我的。

A: I need to go to the bathroom.

B: All right, the restroom's down the hall.

> **A:** 我需要用洗手間。
> **B:** 好的，洗手間往走道下去。

單字

mind	[maɪnd]	v. 介意
bathroom	['bæθˌrum]	浴室；廁所
fidget	['fɪdʒɪt]	坐立難安
rude	[rud]	無禮

英語系列：57

美國老師教你輕鬆說英語

作者／施孝昌
出版者／哈福企業有限公司
地址／新北市板橋區五權街 16 號
電話／(02)2808-6545　傳真／(02) 2808-6545
郵政劃撥／31598840　戶名／哈福企業有限公司
出版日期／2019 年 6 月
定價／NT$ 299 元（附 MP3）

全球華文國際市場總代理／采舍國際有限公司
地址／新北市中和區中山路 2 段 366 巷 10 號 3 樓
電話／(02) 8245-8786　傳真／(02) 8245-8718
網址／www.silkbook.com　新絲路華文網

香港澳門總經銷／和平圖書有限公司
地址／香港柴灣嘉業街 12 號百樂門大廈 17 樓
電話／(852) 2804-6687　傳真／(852) 2804-6409
定價／港幣 100 元（附 MP3）

email ／ haanet68@Gmail.com

郵撥打九折，郵撥未滿 500 元，酌收 1 成運費，
滿 500 元以上者免運費

國家圖書館出版品預行編目資料

美國老師教你輕鬆說英語 / 施孝昌著. -- 新北市：哈
福企業, 2019.06
　面；　公分. --（英語系列；57）
ISBN 978-986-97425-5-9(平裝附光碟片)

1.英語 2.會話

805.188　　　　　　　　　　　　108008697